Angela has three children and now lives in her childhood home where there have always been fairies living in the garden.

Dragon Cottage

Angela Patchett

Dragon Cottage

Nightingale Books

NIGHTINGALE PAPERBACK

A CIP catalogue record for this title is
available from the British Library.

ISBN 978 1 912021 80 2

*Nightingale Books is an imprint of
Pegasus Elliot MacKenzie Publishers Ltd.*
www.pegasuspublishers.com

First Published in 2019

**Nightingale Books
Sheraton House Castle Park
Cambridge England**

Printed & Bound in Great Britain

For Ralph, Hettie and Georgie, with
my love.

Acknowledgements

A big thank you to all my friends and
family for their love and support.

Contents

A secret wish....................................15

No fur and no purr.........................17

Excuse me 19

It does speak 22

Mot..25

The tree house 28

Not a cat 30

If only..36

Sparkles 39

Wondering 42

Easy-peasy 46

Flying 48

Oh no 51

Whoosh! 54

Horror of horrors...........................57

This is my home 60

A nice view......................................62

Look up 65

What's that noise? 68

No more adventures 71

I need a friend 73

Where did he come from? 75

Lost and found 78

Questions... 80

That was close.................................... 84

Out of sight, out of mind 86

Dreaming 89

I just wish he was real 93

Shocked 96

Whoopee! 98

Whatever do you think you're doing?........... 101

Upside down and inside out 105

What if? 108

Off on an adventure 111

Hang on tight! 114

Faster, faster 117

Bubbling mud 120

Keep calm, you can do it................... 122

Dragonland 126

The pearl 129

We're off 133

Wise words 136

Dragon time is different from human time ... 142

Mud on the floor 145

Happy and content 147

No change 149

Where can they be? 152

It was not the right time 155

Dragon Cottage will be no more 157

Dragons are not welcome here.................... 159

I never want to see another dragon.............. 162

It's a bit late now 164

This isn't Dragon Cottage any more 166

What now?.. 170

I wished for a dragon................................ 173

Please don't make him go 176

Can I stay here?....................................... 179

A secret wish

Angelica Rose skipped out of Dragon Cottage. A funny name for a cottage, she thought. I wish a dragon really did live here.

Angelica stopped for a moment. "I wish a real dragon lived here at Dragon Cottage with me."

I won't tell anyone, not even Asha, because he thinks wishing is silly, girls stuff. Angelica loved having an older brother, it was fun, much more fun than having a sister, who would want to play with her toys.

"Come on," Asha called. "No more school for six weeks, we can do what we like now."

"Why did Mum and Dad call it Dragon Cottage?" Angelica asked.

"Oh, I don't know, come on let's go."

"But it's a very strange name," she insisted.

Asha felt cross. "Come on."

Angelica didn't move.

"I think someone called it that two hundred years ago: it's a very old cottage. It wasn't anything to do with Mum and Dad."

"Oh."

"Come on," Asha called. Angelica followed her older brother and forgot all about dragons.

No fur and no purr

The next morning Asha woke up early, no school and lots of free time to do exactly what he wanted to do. The funny thing was, there was so much free time he didn't know what he wanted to do first.

He stretched out in bed and his favourite bear dropped onto the floor.

"Excuse me," a tiny voice squeaked.

Without thinking, Asha said, "Sorry."

Then he thought. My bear has never spoken before. He leaned out of bed and picked up Ted, cuddled him, then looked at him carefully. Ted looked exactly the same as he usually did.

"I'm sorry if you dropped out of bed onto the floor." He stared into Ted's face. Nothing happened. Absolutely nothing at all. He felt rather silly.

He had heard Angelica Rose talking to her dolls and he thought she was really silly… and babyish. And he was a boy, two years older than her and now he was talking to Ted. But it was only because I heard a voice, he reassured himself.

Asha looked at Ted. "Will you talk to me again?" He looked at Ted's face, no movement, not a twitch or a twitter and certainly no words. "Please… please… please… will you say something? You did before, I'm sure you did."

But his pleases didn't work, and he felt even sillier.

"That's it. I'm not going to say another word to you." He rather hoped that may make Ted open his mouth. But it didn't. He put the bear in his usual place on the bed and stretched again. "It's too nice a day to be messing around in here."

But as he stretched out he felt something down the bed, under the duvet, about the size of his cat, Bertie.

"Bertie, what are you doing down there? You usually sleep downstairs."

He put his hand under the duvet to stroke Bertie's fur, but there was no fur, and no purr.

Excuse me

"Whatever is it?" Asha muttered.

"Excuse me," the tiny voice squeaked.

Asha jumped with fright, so frightened he was speechless, so frightened he went running into Angelica's room.

She was fast asleep.

"Wake up. Wake up."

But she didn't move.

"Typical, sisters are never there when you want them, only there when you don't."

But he wasn't going to go back into his own bedroom. He was going to stay right there, until she did wake up. He flung back Angelica's curtains. That might do the trick, he thought.

As the sunlight flooded into the room, she slowly woke up, yawned, stretched, then seeing Asha said sleepily, "Whatever are you doing here?"

"Trying to wake you up."

"What for? There's no school."

"I know. But… but… there's something very strange down my bed and it speaks. It said, 'excuse me'."

"Excuse me! Whatever did it say that for?"

"Don't be silly. I don't know. That's why I'm in here."

"First of all I thought it was Ted, then Bertie. But it's neither and it's not furry."

Angelica stretched out.

"That's exactly what I did and that's when I knew something was there."

Angelica stretched out again. "There's nothing down my bed."

"I know, silly, it's down mine. Are you coming or not?"

Angelica didn't know what to do; she felt frightened, but also excited. Whatever was it? "We could get Mum and Dad."

"They'll still be asleep and they would only say we shouldn't make things up and to go back to sleep."

"I'll come," Angelica said jumping out of bed.

"Hooray, that took a long time," Asha said. "Hurry up."

She followed Asha into his room.

"Look, there it is, under the bedcovers. There's a bump. Can you see it?"

Angelica stared at the duvet. There was a bump. "Let's go to see where Bertie is?"

"I told you, I put my hand down the bed and it wasn't furry."

"What was it?"

"If I knew that, I wouldn't be so frightened, or have come to get you."

"What shall we do? I think we need Mum and Dad. Was it there all night?"

"I don't know, I was asleep."

"But when you woke up could you feel it?"

"No, it's only when it squeaked, 'excuse me'."

Angelica sat on the floor, cross-legged. "Then we need to talk to it and see what happens."

"Why didn't I think of that?" Asha said.

"Because you're not a girl," she giggled.

It does speak

"Excuse me," Asha said. "But who are you?"

"I say excuse me, not you," it squeaked.

Angelica stood back. "It does speak. I thought you may be playing a joke on me and putting your jumper or something under the duvet to tease me."

"Would I do that?"

"Yes," she giggled.

"Excuse me," the voice squeaked again. "What about me?"

The two children stood frozen to the spot, not knowing what to do.

"Didn't you hear me?"

"Y… y… yes," Angelica replied bravely. "But who… or what… are you?"

"I'm not too sure. My skin is covered in an er… er… kind of flowery pattern. I don't think it should be. I think I should be green. I think something went wrong somewhere."

"Do you need any help?" Angelica asked. "We could help you."

There was no reply. No movement from under the duvet and no sound.

"I hope it hasn't gone away," Asha said.

"Me too."

"I don't feel frightened any more."

And then a very strange thing happened.

The duvet moved ever so slightly and then a long flowery tail with a red heart on the end appeared from under the edge of the duvet.

"Whatever's that?" Asha said pointing.

"I don't know. But it must be kind, look at that red heart."

The thing wriggled a bit more under the duvet.

"I've never seen a flowery tail before," Asha said, giggling.

The tail began to move back under the duvet. "Excuse me," it squeaked.

"Oh dear, I think we've upset it now."

"I'm sorry," Asha said.

"I know I should be green but I'm not. I feel really silly and stupid; I don't want you to laugh at me."

"We won't," the children chorused.

"Are you sure?"

"Sure."

And with that the tail appeared again.

This time there was no giggling, only silence.

Angelica walked a little closer. "I think your tail is really pretty. I've never seen a flowery tail before."

"But I'm flowery all over."

"How wonderful."

"You wouldn't like your skin to be covered in flowers."

"I wish it was," Angelica said.

"Be careful what you wish for," it replied.

Then Angelica remembered her secret wish. I wished a dragon lived here with us at Dragon Cottage. Could this be… could this be… our very own dragon? Then she quickly said, "I don't really want to be covered in flowers." She was fearful that her wish may come true.

It heard. "I knew you didn't really like my flowers."

And with that the tail disappeared back under the duvet.

"Oh dear, whatever are we going to do?" Angelica whispered.

Mot

Asha felt brave.

"I'm not frightened any more," he said to Angelica. He threw the duvet back to see what IT really was.

There, curled up in a tight ball was a small creature, its skin covered in a flower pattern, not fur or fluff, with huge eyes looking at him.

"And what are you?" Asha asked.

"I'm a tiny dragon, but something went wrong somewhere. I should have been green, but just look at me."

Angelica stood back in surprise. Her secret wish had come true.

"This really is Dragon Cottage now," she announced.

Asha was speechless.

"How old are you?" Angelica asked.

"In dragon years I'm still very young. I'm hoping when I get a bit older my skin will change to green then I'll feel like a proper dragon."

"You're our very own dragon and that's all that matters."

"I wonder what Mum and Dad will say when we tell them?" Asha said.

"I don't think we should; they may take him away from us."

"I hadn't thought of that."

The dragon began to feel rather special when he knew the children didn't want to lose him.

"He's quite small so we can hide him."

"Yes."

"Will you grow bigger?"

"I don't know, but I would like to be green then I'd feel a lot happier."

Angelica didn't want the dragon to feel sad. "Do you have a name? We can't keep calling you dragon."

"It's Mot. Nice and simple."

"Mot, I like that," Asha said. "Nice and simple like mine. My sister has a very long name, Angelica Rose."

"That is a big name," Mot said. "Bigger than me. Perhaps when I get bigger I'll get a bigger name."

"No, it doesn't work like that," Asha said. "I'm two years older than her."

"I like my name," Angelica said. "And I like yours too, Mot. I can't believe my wish came true. Dragon Cottage has a real dragon living in it now."

"Yes, it looks like I'm here to stay," Mot said happily, stretching out on the bed.

I don't know how we're going to hide Mot from Mum and Dad, Angelica wondered.

The tree house

"The tree house," Angelica announced suddenly.

"What about the tree house?"

"That's where we could hide Mot."

"Excuse me, where are you taking me?"

"You'll love the tree house; it's our secret den. Mum and Dad never go in it and we can come and see you anytime. We won't be going to school for a very long time so we can come every day."

"Where is it?"

"In the garden."

"Let's show him," Asha said.

"Yes, but how do we take Mot there without Mum seeing us?"

"Now we know where we're going we'll just wait until the right time."

"I can walk," Mot said.

"Yes, but it will be quicker if we carry you."

"I can walk quickly."

Angelica laughed. "Up a ladder?"

"What's a ladder?"

"It's how you get into our tree house."

"Are you sure I'm going to like it up in the trees?"

"We do, so I think you will too."

Mot went quiet; he would have to wait and see.

"We'll keep Mot in here under the bedcovers until we know it's safe to take him to the tree house."

"I'll go and see what Mum is doing now. You stay here with Mot," Angelica said. She wandered downstairs and tried to find Mum. Mum was dusting in the lounge.

"Have you come to help me?" Mum grinned.

"No, I was just wondering where you were."

"Why?"

"Oh, just wondering." Angelica didn't want Mum to get suspicious. "It's still raining outside. I hope it won't rain for all of our holidays."

"No, I don't think so: six weeks is a long time. It sounds like you're getting bored already."

"It will be nice to go outside."

"If you're getting bored you can help me in the cellar. I need to carry lots of things up that Dad and I sorted, to take to the charity shop."

"I'm not that bored," Angelica said mischievously, before running upstairs to tell Asha and Mot.

Not a cat

"If Mum's down in the cellar, we could run with Mot outside," Angelica said.

"What about the rain?"

"It's not far to the tree house."

All was quiet downstairs.

"I think we could go now." Angelica ran downstairs to check Mum wasn't around.

"It's clear, come on."

Asha went to pick up Mot. "But how do I pick up a dragon?" he asked.

Angelica looked. "I don't know. Perhaps like picking up Ted or Bertie."

Mot felt worried. "I can walk quickly."

"Yes, but we've got to go down the stairs, then up the tree house ladder. It would be better if I carry you."

Asha tried to pick up Mot like Bertie. Mot felt very different, and it was strange to look down and see a dragon and not a cat in his arms.

"Come on, quick, the coast is clear. I'll go first." Angelica ran quickly down the stairs then beckoned Asha to follow. She flung open the back door and Asha, holding Mot, ran through.

"Has it stopped raining?" Mum shouted from down in the cellar.

"We're just going outside to check!" Angelica shouted, while Asha ran across the garden.

That's a strange thing to do, Mum thought to herself.

"How do I climb up the ladder holding Mot?" Asha asked.

Angelica looked up. "I don't know. I hope Mum doesn't come outside. I think she wonders what we're doing."

"I could get up there myself," Mot said.

"It would be very difficult with four feet," Asha replied.

"Yes, I think you're right," Mot said sadly.

"Quick, you climb up to the top, lean down and I'll try to lift Mot up to you," Angelica said.

Asha put Mot on the ground and ran up. Angelica found it very strange to pick up a real dragon. He didn't feel like anything she'd ever picked up before.

"Quick," Asha called. "Pass him up."

Angelica lifted Mot up as high as she could and Asha leant down as far as he could, but it was quite impossible to do it.

"We've got to be quick," Asha said. "I know, I'll come down again and try to carry him and climb up the ladder with one hand."

"And I'll follow very closely to hold him from behind so he doesn't fall."

"Excuse me, this sounds very unsafe to me," said Mot.

"No, let's try." Asha was already down the ladder and holding Mot.

"Oooh!" Mot cried. "Don't drop me."

"We won't," Angelica tried to reassure him. "We love you; we don't want anything to happen to you."

Mot tried to relax.

Asha climbed the ladder with one hand and Mot was carefully tucked under Asha's other arm. Angelica held his tail.

Just as they were nearing the top of the ladder, Mum shouted out from the back door. "I can see it's stopped raining, but please could you help me carry a box up from the cellar? I can't do it on my own."

"Oh no," Angelica said. "I hope she hasn't seen Mot."

With a great leap and push from behind Mot was in the tree house and safe.

"We'll be there in a few minutes," Angelica called.

"Thanks," Mum replied.

"That was close." Asha shuddered.

Mot looked round. The tree house smelt different from Dragon Cottage, but looked cosy enough. If this was the children's favourite den, it would be good enough for a dragon.

"We better go, we don't want Mum getting suspicious. We'll be back very soon."

"That's all right, it will give me time to look around," Mot replied, feeling very relieved to be safely up the ladder.

Asha and Angelica helped Mum carry the box up from the cellar.

"Thank you," Mum said. "I'm glad you're on holiday."

"That was easier than lifting Mot up the ladder," Asha whispered as they ran across to the tree house. They bounded up the ladder.

"Hello, we're back," Angelica called, looking round for Mot. "Where is he?"

"I hope he hasn't disappeared as quickly as he appeared," Asha said. "I've just become used to him being around."

"I expect he's not far away. Mot, where are you?" she called.

A gentle snore guided them. "Look, he's over there, curled up in the blanket."

Asha's face lit up. "Doesn't he look cute? Do you think he'll be able to live here all the time?"

"It's probably safer at the moment and we can spend as much time here with him as we want."

Mot's snore faded away and he slowly opened one eye. "You're back."

"Yes, I told you we wouldn't be long."

"I've looked round and I like it here. I liked standing outside the door. I can see all over the garden and the cottage from there."

"Oh no," Asha said. "Mum might see you."

"I couldn't see her," Mot said. "So I don't suppose she could see me."

Asha and Angelica didn't know what to say. How on earth could they keep a dragon safe?

"Your flowery skin is a good camouflage," Angelica said thoughtfully.

"I suppose it does have its advantages, but I hope one day it will change to green, then I'll feel like a proper dragon."

"How will that happen?"

"If I knew that I could do it right now," Mot laughed.

And when he laughed Angelica and Asha laughed with him.

"It's no laughing matter you know. I want to be a proper dragon more than anything."

If only

The next morning Asha woke up early. "Come on, Angelica, wake up. We need to see if Mot's all right. It was his first night in the tree house."

Angelica yawned. "I thought you were going to say I had to get up for school."

"No, come on, silly, let's go and see Mot before Mum and Dad wake up."

Angelica stretched, then jumped out of bed excited to see her dragon.

A few minutes later they were up the ladder and in the tree house.

"Look, there he is all curled up on the blanket again."

"It's time to wake up," Asha called cheerily.

Mot opened one eye. "Excuse me, I was fast asleep."

"Sorry," Asha said quickly. "Maybe we should go back to the house."

Asha and Angelica walked slowly across the grass back to the cottage.

"Wherever have you two been?" Mum asked. "Outside in your pyjamas. It must have been important for you two to be up so early."

Asha looked at Angelica and Angelica looked at Asha.

"We thought we'd go and find Bertie."

"But he's over there fast asleep in his basket."

"Oh," Asha said blushing. "When is breakfast?"

"It won't be long."

"We'll go and get dressed," Angelica said. She ran up the stairs with Asha following behind.

"That was close. Do you think she was suspicious?"

"I don't think so."

"Perhaps we shouldn't go to the tree house for a while; we don't want them to wonder."

"I thought they were coming back soon," Mot muttered. He had explored all around the tree house. "I know they said I mustn't go out of the door, but I want to see if they're coming."

Mot stood on the ledge outside the door. He could see all round the garden and also had a full view of the cottage, and the woods beyond. I'd rather be in there, he thought. I'm the dragon they wished for and now I'm not even living in Dragon Cottage but stuck up this tree all on my own. He tried to see Asha and Angelica but couldn't. It wasn't long before he curled up and went to sleep balancing on the ledge outside the door.

Mot woke up, the sun had gone in and it was colder, but still the children hadn't arrived. If only I could get down that ladder I could go and find them myself.

Mot leaned over and looked down the ladder. I'm sure I could, I know I could, and so he put one front foot down, but it wouldn't reach the top rung. He moved sideways. Perhaps I can do it now, but he rocked and shook and nearly fell. Oh no; he looked down and didn't want to fall to the ground. If only I was a proper green dragon I would know what to do. If only I was bigger I would be able to climb down… somehow.

Sparkles

Mot opened one eye and saw little sparkling lights flying round above him. He stretched out and tried to touch one of the sparkles.

"Don't touch me," a tiny voice said. "Who do you think you are sleeping in our house?"

"Asha and Angelica brought me here so I would be safe, but I've been waiting and waiting and they haven't come back to see me."

"They won't, because this is our house."

Mot began to feel frightened. There were a lot of them and only one of him. The sparkles flew round and round above him, some flying so close to his head they nearly touched him. He could feel the fluttering of their wings wafting over his face.

He kept quite still and tried to remind himself that he was a dragon. He may not be green, but he was a dragon.

"I think he's safe, he's quite friendly. I don't think we need to worry," one of them announced. The biggest one.

"I'm glad you said that," Mot replied. "I won't hurt you."

"We won't hurt you either."

"What are you?"

One of the sparkles chuckled and another giggled. "We're fairies and what are you?"

"I'm Mot the dragon. One of the children who live in Dragon Cottage wished for a dragon, and before I knew it, I was here. The only problem is, I'm not a grown-up dragon yet. My skin should be green all over and I should be able to fly, I think. I've got wings so I suppose I can. You seem to be able to fly; perhaps you could help me?"

"It's easy-peasy." One of the fairies flew round and round just above his face; stopping right on the end of his nose. "Can you see me better now?"

Mot's eyes focused on the tiny fairy. "You're very pretty and I like your happy smile."

"We are happy," another said. "It's nice living here."

"Do you know the children?" Mot asked.

"Yes, we've seen them coming to play here, but they don't know we're here. We have so much fun watching them though."

Wondering

"You can fly and you will," the fairy called.

"But I can't. Is it because my skin isn't green? Is it because my wings aren't strong enough?"

"Don't keep worrying and wondering, just watch us. Perhaps you should pretend you're a fairy and not a dragon."

Mot began to laugh. He looked down at his skin. "Perhaps I should wear a fairy dress."

The fairies started to giggle. "I don't think that would help. You're all right just as you are."

Mot's wing began to lift upwards, then the other, but he didn't lift off the ground. "Maybe I'm too heavy to fly. I'm not little like you."

"You can and you will," one of the fairies repeated. "I think it may be better if we went to the ledge outside by the door. Perhaps you could take off from there."

"That's a good idea," Mot said. He walked towards the ledge, then looked down. "Oh dear, what if my wings don't work? It's a long way down."

"Our wings work and yours will too."

"Are you sure?" Mot trembled.

At that very moment Mot saw the children running over the grass towards the tree house.

"What are you doing outside?" Asha called.

"Trying to fly."

"Oh no. Are you going to leave us? Fly off and never come back."

"Dragons fly, so if I am to be a real and proper dragon I must fly."

"Oh no," Angelica said sadly.

"Perhaps it's not such a good idea for Mot to be living in the tree house," Asha whispered.

"But where else can we hide him?"

"If he's in the cottage we can keep an eye on him and he won't be lonely."

"He could sleep under my bed; I haven't got anything under there at all," Angelica said excitedly. "Mum and Dad won't find him."

"Why didn't we think of that before?" Asha said.

"How do we carry him back down the ladder? It was difficult getting him up, but it will be even harder getting him down."

"We'll wake up really early," Asha suggested. "Then we can make sure Mot is installed in his new home under your bed before Mum and Dad are up. We're going to take you back into Dragon Cottage tomorrow," Asha announced.

"Thank goodness for that. How can I ever be a proper dragon living out in the garden in a tree house? It's bad enough having a flowery skin and not being able to fly, but to not live in Dragon Cottage is an insult."

"We only brought you out here because we thought you'd be safe and that you'd be happy."

"It's a pity you didn't think of under Angelica's bed earlier. It would have saved a lot of problems."

But that night, Mot's last night in the tree house, he began to feel sad when he saw the twinkling lights in the darkness flying around him. "I'm going to miss you and how will I ever learn to fly if I don't see you again?"

One of the larger fairies flew very near to his nose. "We can fly anywhere, so there's no reason why we can't fly over to Dragon Cottage to see you."

"Oh, will you? Please."

"Yes of course, because we'll miss you too."

Mot shut his eyes and before his gentle snore began he wondered what new adventures he was going to have.

Easy-peasy

Mot didn't quite know how the children managed to get him down the ladder and into his new home under Angelica's bed, but they had. He remembered the fairies' words and hoped they would come to visit him soon. He wanted to fly and he knew they were the only ones to help him.

"I hope Mum doesn't wonder why we're spending such a long time in your room," Asha said.

"I think Mot is very safe under my bed. It's pushed right up against the wall in the corner so there is lots of space for him."

"But if you hear Mum or Dad coming into my room you must be quiet, Mot, even if we're here, because they'll wonder who we are talking to."

"Please come to see me more than you did in the tree house because I don't like being alone for too long." Then he remembered the fairies… he hadn't been lonely for long. He wondered how they would find their way to Angelica's bedroom.

"Asha, Angelica," Dad called up the stairs.

"Oh no, not again."

"It doesn't matter now," Angelica said. "We've managed to get Mot back into Dragon Cottage and he's safely in his new home. Come on let's go and have our breakfast. We'll be back soon."

The bedroom was quiet; very quiet except for a fluttering of wings. Mot recognised the sound. It's the fairies, he thought. He peered out from under the bed and to his delight he saw lots of sparkles flying round the room. "How did you know where I was?"

"Easy-peasy, one of us followed, then when she knew where you were she flew back to tell us."

"Did anyone see you flying into the house?"

"No one sees us fairies."

"Why is that? I can," Mot asked.

"But you're a dragon. If humans don't believe in fairies they can't see them."

"I want you to teach me how to fly. You will, won't you?"

"Of course, we said we will and we will."

Flying

"Do you think Mot can sleep on my bed?" Angelica asked Asha.

"I don't know. What happens if Mum and Dad come in?"

Mot heard. "I could sleep under the duvet. Don't forget when I arrived you found me under Asha's duvet."

"Yes, but you must keep your tail under the duvet. If Mum and Dad see a red heart hanging down they'll take a look to see where it's coming from."

Mot, Angelica and Asha giggled.

"And we don't want them saying we can't keep you. That's why we moved you to the tree house."

"Could I sit on the bed now?" Mot asked.

Angelica picked him up. He looked down from the bed. This was a good height to fly, he thought. Not as scary as from the tree house and, if his wings didn't work, it would be a soft landing on the carpet.

In the middle of the night when all was quiet and dark, Mot pushed the duvet back until he could crawl out and sit on top of it. He saw lots of sparkles all around him. "Do you want to try to fly?"

"Yes, but how do I do it?"

One fairy sat next to Mot on the edge of the bed. "Watch me." She just flew. "It's as simple as that."

"Don't forget I'm bigger and a lot heavier than you."

She giggled. "Don't forget your wings are bigger."

Mot felt confident, flapped his wings and began to fly. He didn't fall and land on the carpet. He just flew. "Wow, I'm flying, I'm flying!" he called.

Angelica opened an eye to see lots of sparkling lights flying round her bedroom, but to her utter surprise Mot was flying above her.

"Oh no, how did you get up there? Someone might see you; you're supposed to be hiding so Mum and Dad don't see you and take you away."

"I'm the dragon of Dragon Cottage, no one can take me away and I'm flying. I'm a proper dragon now. It doesn't matter if my skin is flowery. I'm a real dragon and I feel great."

Angelica ran very, very quietly into Asha's room. "Wake up, come and see Mot. Whatever are we going to do now?"

Asha jumped out of bed and when he saw Mot flying near the ceiling he couldn't believe his eyes. "How will we ever manage to hide him now?"

But Mot was having the time of his life and called down from his great height, "Don't you wish you could fly like me?"

Oh no

"How did you fly?" Asha asked.

"My friends taught me. Look, we're all flying."

Asha looked harder. The room was full of sparkles.

"We're fairies, not sparkles, we're Mot's friends."

Angelica felt very excited. She had believed in fairies, but never seen one before.

"What made you all come into my bedroom?"

"Because we're Mot's friends and he wanted us to teach him to fly. We live in the tree house. Your tree house."

"We've never seen you in the tree house," Asha said.

"No, but I did," Mot called.

"I wish we could fly like Mot and the fairies."

"Maybe you will grow wings too," a fairy called.

"Don't forget I already had wings. I had never been able to fly because I didn't know how until I met you."

Angelica looked at Asha quite expecting to see he had grown wings. But he hadn't.

"How are you going to get down? If Mum comes into my bedroom in the morning and sees you all flying round she'll say you can't live here."

"She's got to catch me first," Mot called feeling very powerful and excited.

"Oh no, what can we do?"

"I don't know, I just don't know, but I feel excited, perhaps we will fly too."

But Angelica and Asha didn't suddenly grow wings. Eventually Mot felt tired and landed back on the bed. "I didn't know how to fly, and I have never landed before but it's easy-peasy, just like one of my fairy friends told me."

"Thank goodness you're safely down again. It will soon be time for breakfast. Please can you go back to your home under the bed, so Mum and Dad don't say you can't live here with us any more. We don't want to lose you."

But hiding Mot seemed to be getting harder and harder and more worrying by the minute.

"What about the fairies?" Asha said seriously.

"We can fly back to our home in the tree house. There are lots of windows open and we know our way now."

"You will come back again, won't you?" Mot asked. "Now you've taught me to fly, you will come back."

One little fairy chuckled. "Now you can fly you can come to see us."

"Oh yes, I hadn't thought of that."

But Angelica and Asha sighed.

"Oh no, whatever is Mot going to do next?"

Whoosh!

The sun shone brighter, the days became hotter, and Mot settled in his new home under the bed. The fairies hadn't flown back to see him yet and he was missing them… giving him more flying lessons.

Angelica and Asha were in the garden playing with some friends. Mum walked into first Angelica's, then Asha's bedroom and flung the windows open wide. Mot heard her footsteps and stayed very still and quiet under the bed as he had been told, but when the room was quiet he poked his face out from under the bed.

He smelt fresh air; the smell of freedom. Within a few minutes he was sitting on the window sill looking up and down. "I wonder if I could," he murmured. "Yes, I think I could." He flapped his wings and decided to fly around the bedroom first as a trial to make sure he could still do it. He remembered, and soon he was flying around the room, higher and higher, until suddenly with one big whoosh! he was out of the window and flying outside.

He didn't look down in case he lost his nerve. He saw the tree house and headed straight for it. He spotted the children far below him; he hoped they couldn't see him and flew as fast as he could.

How do I land? he thought. I must land in the tree house, not on the ground. Fortunately, the door was wide open and he flew straight through.

"H… h… how do I land?"

"Watch me," one of the fairies said. It was not many minutes before he was safely down.

"I can't believe my eyes," another fairy said. "You have done well and all on your own."

Mot felt happy and proud.

"Have you come back to stay with us?"

"I saw the bedroom window wide open; I flapped my wings and here I am. Do you think I can manage to get back to Dragon Cottage?"

"Don't worry, we can come with you."

"I'd like to be here with you for a while, then I'll fly back later."

"You sound very confident about your flying."

"Do I?"

"Yes, and so you should; flying all that way on your own."

"You're not flowery all over," one fairy noticed. "Parts of your body have turned green."

"Whatever's happening to me?" Mot asked. "I do feel a bit different."

Horror of horrors

Angelica ran up to her room and looked under the bed for Mot. To her horror he was not there. Horror of horrors, the bedroom window was wide open.

She ran to find Asha. He was standing in the kitchen with Dad. She tried to attract his attention; with no luck. She ran into the garden to see if she could see Mot. She stood under the open bedroom window expecting to find him on the grass.

"I don't want my lovely dragon to go. He can't leave Dragon Cottage; he just can't."

Then she heard a fluttering, rustling sound and looked up to see Mot flying with lots of sparkly fairies flying next to him.

"Oh, Mot, I thought I'd never see you again."

He flew towards the open bedroom window and disappeared. Angelica ran as fast as her legs would carry her. There was Mot lying on the bed after making a safe landing. The fairies were all flying round and round the bedroom. She flung her arms round him, tears stinging her eyes.

"Look at him, look," one of the fairies called.

"Yes, I think I look different," Mot said feeling a little embarrassed.

Angelica stood back. "You've changed colour, you're not flowery all over any more. How did that happen?"

"I don't know. Do I look good?"

"Oh yes."

"Perhaps something happens to Mot when he flies," a fairy suggested.

Mot began to feel proud of his adventure.

Asha walked in. "I see the fairies are back."

"Yes, they came with Mot. Mum opened the window and he flew out."

"Oh no, where did you go?"

"I flew to the tree house to see the fairies because I wanted them to give me more flying lessons."

"He didn't need any," one fairy said. "He flew all the way to the tree house on his own."

"Yes, I looked down and saw you playing with your friends," said Mot.

"We didn't see you, but more importantly Mum and Dad didn't see you."

"What are we going to do now?" Angelica asked, looking very worried.

"I just don't know." Asha walked over to the open window and shut it very firmly.

"Don't forget we need to go home," a fairy called.

"Yes, but Mot is not going with you. No more adventures for him. I'll open the little window to let you out when you want to go."

"How do I look?" Mot asked.

Asha stared hard. "Parts of you are green now. How did that happen?"

"No one knows," a fairy replied.

"But I've been told I look very nice."

"Let's hold him up in front of the mirror then he'll see," Angelica said.

Mot looked in the mirror. "I look very different. I wonder what will happen next?"

This is my home

Angelica woke in the night to hear a very familiar and reassuring snore coming from under the bed. She saw some fairies flying and sparkling round the bedroom. "I'm glad you stayed here. How can we keep Mot safe?"

"He is safe, he was safe. He knew he could fly and he could, and he came back to Dragon Cottage. This is his home now, with you."

"But Mum and Dad may say he can't stay here with us, if they find him."

"Even if they do, Mot will find a way back here… somehow."

"I hope you're right."

Several fairies sat on the pillow next to Angelica and she soon fell asleep.

In the morning the fairies asked if she could open the little window so they could fly out. As they flew away, Angelica tried to remind herself

that Mot would always live at Dragon Cottage –
whatever happened, and the fairies would come
back soon.

Mot crawled out from under the bed when he
heard the window shut.

"The fairies have gone home, but they will
come back soon. They told me you will always live
at Dragon Cottage. Is that true?" Angelica asked
anxiously.

"Yes, I am the dragon of Dragon Cottage. This
is my home and whatever happens, or wherever I
go, I will always come back… probably flying!"
Mot laughed. "How do I look?"

"The same as yesterday; nothing's changed."

"I don't know how I stopped being flowery all
over. I wish the rest of me would change. Perhaps
if I do some more flying I will."

Oh no, Angelica thought. Where's he going
this time?

A nice view

Dragon Cottage was quiet. Mot peered out from under the bed. He was disappointed when he saw that the window was tightly shut. He felt brave. He couldn't hear any voices and decided to explore the cottage. He went into Asha's bedroom. He looked at the window – it was closed.

"There must be a way out," Mot muttered wondering whether he dare go into Mum and Dad's bedroom. But the smell of fresh air, of freedom, was stronger than his fear, and before he knew it he was inside the bedroom and sitting on the window sill next to the wide-open window. He spotted Mum, Dad, Angelica and Asha on the grass below. I'll fly the other way, he thought, out to the front. He flapped his wings and he was off.

One of the fairies sitting by the door of the tree house saw something flying in the air. It must be

Mot. He's off again, she thought. She called to the others, "Mot's on another adventure."

Several of the fairies flew outside to look. "Can you see him? He's right over there."

"I'm going to join him," one of the fairies replied.

"Me too," another called.

"You'll have to be quick because he's flying rather fast," she giggled.

It wasn't many minutes before several of the fairies were flying off to join Mot.

Mot was very surprised to be joined by his fairy friends. "I didn't think anyone had seen me?"

"I'm sure the humans didn't spot you, but don't forget we're fairies. Where are you going?"

"I don't know."

"We're coming with you to make sure you're all right."

"Of course, I'm all right. I don't need anyone," and with that Mot accelerated.

"Our wings aren't as big as yours," one of the fairies called.

"They may be smaller, but we're quite as quick as Mot," another said.

But Mot quickly became tired. I need to rest, he thought, but where am I going to land? He circled around and looked back at the cottage.

Time to go back, he thought. He turned around and headed home with the fairies flying around him. As he got nearer, he saw the chimney of Dragon Cottage sticking up above the thatched roof. That's where I can land, he thought. I can rest there for a while. I don't want to fly back into Mum and Dad's bedroom because they may be there.

"What's he doing now?" one of the fairies called, seeing Mot heading for the chimney. "I do believe he's going to land on it."

And with one almighty swoop Mot was standing on top of the chimney feeling very proud of himself.

"I hope Mum and Dad don't see him."

"If they do look up they won't believe their eyes if they see a dragon sitting on top of the chimney of Dragon Cottage."

One of the fairies looked down. "I can't see Mum and Dad in the back garden now, only the children."

"That's all right then."

A fairy joined Mot on the chimney.

"We've got a nice view from here; I must remember to do this more often," Mot said.

Look up

Asha and Angelica ran into her bedroom.

"I'm sorry we've been so long," Angelica said looking under the bed. But to her horror, Mot was not there. "Oh no, wherever is he now?"

Asha looked at the window; it was tightly shut. Then they ran into his room; the window was shut. "Oh no, where is he? I hope Mum and Dad don't find him." Asha looked through the doorway into their bedroom.

"Are you all right?" Mum asked.

"Yes, I wondered where you were?"

"Did you want anything?"

"No." Asha saw that their window was wide open and ran back to tell Angelica.

"Mum and Dad's window is wide open. Do you think he flew out of there, or do you think he's somewhere in the cottage?"

"Oh no," Angelica said. "I wish he'd stay still, or at least tell us what he's doing."

"Where do we look first?" Asha checked his bedroom, then they went into the bathroom, then looked in every room downstairs.

"I think he must be outside," Angelica said. "Let's go and try the tree house. He may have gone to see the fairies."

They climbed up the ladder full of hope, but Mot was not there. They sat in the doorway feeling very sad, looking round the garden for any sign of Mot.

"I hope the fairies were right that Mot will come back to Dragon Cottage."

Angelica looked at the cottage hoping above all hope she would see him again.

She looked upwards and there, to her amazement, perched on the very top of the chimney was Mot. She began to giggle. "You'll never guess where he is. Look over there."

Asha looked. "Where?"

"Look up."

"Oh no, he's on top of the chimney. He looks a bit bigger and a slightly different colour."

"But how do we get him down and how do we get him back into the cottage without Mum and Dad seeing him?"

What's that noise?

Mot looked down at the children far below him. He began to feel frightened. What if I can't manage to get down? he thought. He started to wobble.

"Oh no!" Asha cried. "He's going to fall."

"I hope he doesn't fall down the chimney."

"He won't do that. Look he's grown, he's too big now."

"If he's too big to fall down the chimney he will be too big to hide under my bed again."

Mot wobbled more and more.

"Oh no, why doesn't he fly?" Asha said.

"Perhaps he can only fly up, not down."

"But he has landed before."

Angelica saw a tiny fairy flying around Mot. "I think she's trying to help him."

"I wish he'd hurry up and fly. I'm getting worried he may fall down the thatched roof and hurt himself if he doesn't do something soon. I'm going to shout to him."

"Dad may hear you."

"I can't see Dad around. Flap your wings, fly!" Asha shouted.

Mot lifted his wings. The fairy flew around him but Mot had lost his nerve. He was at the greatest height he had ever been. Much higher than when he was sitting on the ledge of the tree house. Mot couldn't and wouldn't move.

"It's tea time. Come on, you two!" Mum shouted from the kitchen.

"Oh no, he may fall, we can't leave him stuck on the top of the chimney."

"Come on! Your tea will be getting cold!" Mum shouted.

"I'm not going," Asha said. "I can't leave him."

"I'll go and tell Mum you're not hungry," said Angelica.

"She will never believe that. What if she comes out into the garden and sees Mot?"

"We'll just have to go in," Angelica said sadly.

Asha stuffed his tea into his mouth as quickly as he could."

"You are hungry," Mum said. "Be careful you don't choke."

"Whatever's that noise?" Dad asked standing up. "It sounded like it was coming from the chimney."

Oh no, Asha thought, whatever has Mot done now?

"I didn't hear anything," Angelica said, hoping above all hope that Dad would believe her.

"Sit down and eat your tea," Mum said.

"Are you sure you didn't hear anything, Angelica?"

Before she could reply, Mum said, "If it's anything important you will hear it again."

Dad looked at his tea. It looked far more tempting than going outside to look at the chimney.

I hope Mot hasn't slid down the roof and hurt himself, Asha worried.

No more adventures

After what seemed like the longest teatime ever, Asha and Angelica escaped to the garden.

Asha looked up at the chimney, but to his horror Mot was not there. "Where's he gone?"

"If only I knew."

Then, a tiny voice from behind them said, "Why are you looking up at the chimney when I'm sitting over here?"

Sure enough, there sat Mot looking a little dishevelled, much smaller then he'd looked on top of the chimney, in fact, much smaller than he'd ever been.

"Oh dear, oh dear, what am I to do?" Mot said. "I started to slide down the roof, then suddenly my wings started to work again and I flew all the way down to the ground. But look at me now."

"You look fine to me," Angelica said kindly.

"But one minute I felt like a proper, grown up dragon. Then as soon as I landed, I kind of shrank. It was very worrying, I wondered when it would stop. I feared I would disappear altogether."

"Yes, you are smaller than before," Asha said.

"Shh," Angelica said putting her finger to her lips. "I'm glad you are smaller. I was worried that you wouldn't ever fit under my bed again."

Mot smiled. "I hadn't thought of that. I'd like to go under the bed right now. I feel a bit shaken up."

"Thank goodness for that," Angelica whispered. "Perhaps now he will stay safely inside Dragon Cottage." She scooped him up and held him tightly in her hands.

Asha walked over to the house. "I'll go and check where Mum and Dad are, then we'll take him back upstairs."

And it was not many minutes before Mot was curled up under Angelica's bed, sleeping happily. He was so very happy that he was not stuck up on the chimney any more. In fact, as he was going to sleep he told himself he was never ever going on an adventure again.

I need a friend

Mot woke up in the middle of the night. Angelica's room was very dark. It felt strange being so small… and lonely. I wish I knew some more dragons, he thought. It's very nice in Dragon Cottage, but I need a friend: someone like me. If I'm not going on any more adventures it's going to get boring.

I wonder if… I wonder if I could climb onto Angelica's bed. I don't like it here under the bed now I'm so small. I could sit on the duvet… just until the morning when she wakes up. Mot tried to climb onto the bed. It seemed so high, much, much too high.

There's only one way up and that's to fly. I'm sure I can do it again, he told himself. He flapped his tiny wings and he was off, flying upwards to Angelica's duvet. But as he flew he began to get larger. By the time he had landed on the duvet he was back to his normal size. I wonder how that happened? he pondered. If only I could work out how to get bigger and smaller I could do it whenever I wanted. Like now. I don't want to be larger because Mum and Dad might see me. Well, there's only one thing to do, I'll have to hide under the duvet now I'm up here because I don't fancy flying down again. He shuddered when he remembered how he had started falling off the chimney. Whatever would have happened to him if his wings hadn't worked. He snuggled under the duvet feeling comforted that he was not alone. No more adventures for me. I'm staying here, he thought.

Angelica tossed and turned restlessly, dreaming that she had lost Mot forever.

I wish she'd keep still, Mot thought, I'm beginning to think it would be more comfortable under the bed. Eventually, Mot's tiredness overtook him and he went into a deep sleep like Angelica. So deep that neither of them woke at their normal time. They continued sleeping and sleeping and didn't hear Mum calling from downstairs that breakfast was ready. And they didn't hear Mum's footsteps pounding up the stairs, or opening the bedroom door, or saying 'breakfast's ready'. They didn't wake up until Mum pulled the duvet back and said, "Come on, lazybones, breakfast's on the table."

Where did he come from?

Asha sat at the kitchen table eating his breakfast wondering why Angelica was sleeping so soundly. However, he had no worries when Mum went upstairs as he believed Mot was smaller than his usual size and tucked safely under the bed.

"Your breakfast's ready downstairs," Mum said again.

Angelica rubbed her eyes.

"Come on, sleepy head."

Angelica's eyes began to focus as she woke up and to her horror saw Mot curled up.

"I didn't know you had a toy dragon," Mum said. "I thought you had a bear and a rabbit, but not a dragon. Where did he come from?"

Mot kept very, very still, hardly daring to breathe and keeping his eyes tightly closed.

Angelica jumped out of bed. "Did you say breakfast's ready. I'm coming," she said hoping to distract Mum.

"He looks very nice. Fancy you having a dragon. It's just what we need here in Dragon Cottage."

Mot nearly smiled a very happy dragon smile but managed to keep still. If Mum wants me here, what's all the fuss been about? If only she knew I was real.

"Come on, Mum, let's go downstairs now."

Mum took a long, lingering look at the dragon before leaving the room. Mot was as still as still could be. But Mum said, "It's very strange, but your dragon toy looks almost real."

"As real as my bear and hop hop rabbit," Angelica said. "Come on, Mum."

Asha looked at Angelica's face when she sat down at the breakfast table. He could see that something was wrong, very wrong, but he didn't know what.

After breakfast, Asha said, "Let's go and play upstairs."

"Yes," Angelica replied quickly.

"Going to see your dragon again?" Mum asked.

Asha's face dropped. How could Mum possibly know about Mot?

"Tell me, tell me. What's going on?" Asha whispered as they ran up the stairs.

But Angelica was in her bedroom before she could reply. She looked on the bed. Mot was not there. "Oh no, where is he now? I do wish he'd stay in one place. Now Mum knows."

"Knows what?"

"Mot was in my bed under the duvet. I didn't know and when Mum threw back the covers she found him. She thinks he's a toy like bear and hop hop."

"Are you sure?"

"No. But parents don't expect toys to be real."

"I hope not."

"But that's not the biggest problem now. We need to find Mot, and quickly before he gets into more trouble."

Lost and found

Asha and Angelica hunted high and low but couldn't find Mot anywhere.

"Do you think he's flown off outside again?"

"He did say he wasn't going on any more adventures."

"I know, but he flew up onto my bed and we told him to stay under the bed, not on it," Angelica said. "Mum did say that what we need at Dragon Cottage is a dragon. She may be pleased."

"But she thinks he's a toy, not real," Asha said.

"Let's find him first then worry about that later."

Wherever they hunted they couldn't find Mot.

"Do you think he's left the cottage or has gone back to the tree house?"

"I can't see how he's got out. All the windows are shut, but you can never be sure with a dragon, particularly one like Mot." Angelica giggled nervously.

"Come on, let's go outside and look."

They walked downstairs through the kitchen and outside. No sign of Mum or Dad, and no sign of Mot. They climbed the ladder to the tree house. No Mot and no fairy sparkles. It was completely empty.

"Perhaps he's on the chimney again," Asha suggested.

"Oh no, I hadn't thought of that. He did say no more adventures, but you can never be too sure with Mot."

Asha and Angelica stood on the lawn and looked up. No Mot on the chimney or roof.

"I feel relieved," Asha said.

"But at least if he was on the chimney again we would know where he was."

"He must be in the cottage somewhere."

They walked through the back door into the kitchen. Mum sat on one chair round the table. Dad sat on one chair round the table and there sat Mot on another chair. Larger than he had been on the bed. Sitting there quite comfortably.

Asha and Angelica couldn't believe their eyes.

Questions

"I went upstairs to find your toy dragon to show Dad. He looks so real," Mum said.

"We're glad you have got him. Who gave him to you?" Dad asked.

"We thought we could have him as the cottage mascot," Mum said. "But of course, you could still play with him."

Asha and Angelica didn't utter a word. Shocked to find Mot, but even more shocked to hear Mum and Dad's words. Asha quickly realised that Mum and Dad didn't know he was real, but Angelica just kept staring at Mot hoping he wouldn't move or speak.

"When I carried him downstairs he felt so real; he was warm. Where do you put the batteries in him?"

Angelica didn't know whether to laugh, cry or run away and hide as quickly as possible. But she stayed rooted to the spot: speechless.

"Where did you find him?" Asha asked, not able to hide his surprise.

"In Angelica's room, of course."

'But where?' Asha nearly said, but just managed to stop himself.

"You sound surprised," Mum said slowly.

"Oh no," Asha said quickly.

Angelica was surprised to see Mot bigger than he had been on her bed; she wondered what he had been doing and where in her room Mum had found him. But she was much more worried that he may move or show any signs of being real. If Mum and Dad found out she was sure they wouldn't allow him to live there any more.

"He's such an unusual colour. He's not like a normal dragon; they're green all over. He's got flowery skin on his tummy," Dad said.

"This is a most unusual cottage," Mum replied. "An unusual dragon lives in an unusual cottage."

Mot felt himself getting hot inside. I just want to be a normal, green all over, dragon. I don't want to be unusual even if I live in an unusual cottage, he thought to himself.

"Where did you say he came from?" Dad asked Angelica.

Asha decided he had to do something… and quick. "I think Mot needs to go back upstairs to

Angelica's bedroom. That's where he belongs," he said crossly.

"I didn't know his name was Mot," Mum replied. "What's the rush? He's quite all right here with us."

That was close

Asha and Angelica sat in her bedroom with Mot.

"Phew, that was close," Asha said. "I knew I had to do something quickly."

"One minute I was sitting in the kitchen. The next I was grabbed and now we're back up here," Mot said. "I felt very cross when they said I was an unusual dragon. I felt so angry I could feel myself getting hotter and hotter. But I kind of think they like me, even if I'm not green all over."

"I think they do like you, but they don't know you're real. If they knew you are not a stuffed toy they wouldn't let you live here."

"Mum said I could be the cottage mascot. It sounds very important. I would like to be important."

"It's really important you stay under the bed and hopefully Mum and Dad will forget all about you. Where were you when Mum found you?"

"I was wandering round your bedroom just wondering if there was somewhere better to hide than under the bed. I heard some footsteps and I kept very, very still. Then I was scooped up by Mum, carried down the stairs and then she sat me on the chair in the kitchen. I kept very, very still. It was difficult, but I did it. I want to stay in Dragon Cottage."

"If you stay under the bed Mum won't see you there, so she'll forget all about you."

"We hope," Asha said solemnly.

"Oh dear," Mot sighed. "I don't like being forgotten and I don't like being under the bed. It's dark and there's not much space. If only I could be a proper green dragon and do what I like."

"It won't be forever," Asha said.

"I jolly well hope not," Mot replied.

Out of sight, out of mind

"Please will you stay under the bed tonight?" Angelica asked.

Mot looked sad. "It's dark and there's not much space for a growing dragon."

"I hope you don't grow too big too quickly."

But Mot secretly hoped he would grow and that he would become a proper green dragon soon. The only problem was he liked it in Dragon Cottage and he wanted to stay… forever. If only he knew how to do both.

Angelica turned the light out. "I'll see you in the morning, hopefully under my bed not in it." She smiled.

Mot curled up into a ball under the bed and slept all night… dreaming about flying and being green all over and being loved by everyone in Dragon Cottage.

Asha walked into Angelica's bedroom early in the morning, before Mum and Dad were awake, and looked under the bed to see if Mot was still there. He was and fast asleep.

Oh good, he thought, and went back to bed and to sleep.

Mum and Dad didn't mention Mot at breakfast time and Asha and Angelica hoped he was now forgotten. Out of sight, out of mind.

But Mot did not want to be forgotten and did not want to stay under the bed. He wanted to be downstairs with the rest of the family.

Asha and Angelica were playing in the garden. The house was quiet and Mum went quietly up the stairs and then into Angelica's bedroom. She looked around, but could not see a dragon.

That's strange, she thought, then wandered into Asha's bedroom. She looked all around, but could not see Mot. She walked back into Angelica's room and pulled back the duvet, expecting to see him, but no, he was not there. Mum looked at Angelica's bear and hop hop rabbit, but there was no dragon with them. Perhaps I imagined seeing a dragon. "I wish we had a real dragon living here with us in Dragon Cottage. What fun it would be," Mum said loudly.

Mot heard her words from his hiding place under the bed. 'I'm here', he nearly said, but just managed to stop himself, remembering what Asha and Angelica had told him.

Mot could hear Mum's footsteps slowly disappearing down the stairs. He felt sad and didn't know what to do. Eventually, he thought there was absolutely nothing he could do and went to sleep.

Dreaming

Mot slept under Angelica's bed and dreamt that he was flying. The strangest thing was that he was not flying alone. He was bigger than he'd ever been and he had a passenger on his back. He couldn't quite see who it was. Then he woke up.

Mot wanted to see more, and he tried to go to sleep again to continue the dream. However hard he tried he could not sleep, nor dream.

Fancy that, Mot thought, me flying with a passenger. However could I do that when I'm not going to have any more adventures ever again. Then he wondered how big he could grow. I must be able to grow really big. I wonder how I can do that? I'm certainly not going to get very big sitting under this bed and I did hear Mum say what fun it would be if I was a real dragon. I heard her with my own ears. I wonder… I wonder…

Mot crawled out from under the bed and looked round the room. All was quiet. The window was shut so there was no chance of an adventure. Or was there? I know I shouldn't, but I think I've changed my mind. I do want another adventure.

Downstairs Dad said, "The fair is in town."

"Do we really have to go to the fair?" Asha whined.

"I can't understand it," Dad replied. "You used to be whining about how much longer it would be before we could go. The fair comes to town once a year, so we need to make the most of it while it is here."

But Asha had other things on his mind… like being with Mot, and making sure Mum and Dad forgot him.

"We'll be going in ten minutes so make sure you're ready."

Angelica and Asha ran up the stairs and into her bedroom.

"Where's Mot?"

They saw his tail, or rather the red heart on the end of it, sticking out from under the bed.

"Oh no," Asha said. "It's getting quite impossible trying to hide him."

Mot was fast asleep and snoring very gently. Angelica tucked his tail under the bed. "He'll be all right now. Come on, we had better go. We don't want Dad wondering what we're doing up here."

Downstairs Mum sat down in her favourite armchair, hoping for a few hours of peace and quiet. The house seemed very still and after a little snooze she began to miss everyone. Maybe I should have gone to the fair with them, it might have been fun. She started to remember when she was a child and how she had loved going to the fair. In fact, it had been one of the highlights of her summer. She sat staring out of the window of Dragon Cottage remembering when she was a little girl. Perhaps it's not too late; perhaps I could get on a bus and go to the fair myself.

"Yes, that's exactly what I'll do," she muttered. With that she stood up and quickly went upstairs to get changed. As she passed Angelica's room she saw something that intrigued her. Something red and looking rather heart-shaped was sticking out from under the bed. I wonder what Angelica's left there, she thought, and she went to investigate. As she bent down to touch it, it disappeared back under the bed.

Mot had heard footsteps, woken up and quickly curled himself up into a ball, hiding just as Asha had told him to do.

But it was too late. Mum bent down to get a better view under the bed and saw it belonged to a dragon. The same dragon that she had seen before. Then she remembered what she had come upstairs for… to get changed so she could go to the fair. She didn't know what to do now. She was intrigued how a stuffed toy dragon could move its tail. Mum stood there staring, and Mot kept as still as still could be.

I just wish he was real

Mum sat in Angelica's bedroom on the floor cross-legged; something she hadn't done for a very long time, just staring at Mot.

He knew he had to keep very, very still; it grew harder and harder and he just hoped above all hopes she would soon walk away. But she didn't.

Mum's thoughts of going to the fair had completely disappeared. She watched Mot very closely to try to see how a toy could look so lifelike and how he had moved his tail. She stared and stared but nothing happened. Her legs began to ache sitting on the floor.

"I just wish this dragon would do something. I just wish he was real. What fun it would be if he was. He could be called the dragon of Dragon Cottage and then we would all be happy." She tried to stand up but her legs felt numb. She looked down at her apron which she hadn't taken off after cooking. Her oven gloves were still draped over her shoulder. She looked at her watch. "Gosh is that really the time?" she muttered. "I don't think there will be time to go to the fair now." So, she slowly walked back downstairs.

Mot, hearing her footsteps disappearing, felt a little sad. He began to wonder what it would be like to be THE dragon of Dragon Cottage. He heard Mum say everyone would be happy. Including me, Mot thought, and I'm not very happy hiding under this bed. The smell of adventure filled his nostrils. The thought of being happy and important made him quiver. With that, he boldly came out from under the bed and he stood in the middle of the room. He could hear Mum downstairs.

I wonder if I could get down these stairs? I'm sure it would be easier than the tree house ladder. He walked out of the bedroom and stood at the top of the stairs looking down. To his amazement he saw Mum standing at the bottom of the stairs looking up.

Shocked

"How did you get there?" Mum asked not expecting a reply.

"I walked," Mot said.

Mum was so shocked she had to steady herself by holding on to the stair rail.

"You said you wished I was real then everyone would be happy. I am, so what's the problem?" Mot said very boldly.

Mum stood still just staring up the stairs not able to reply.

Oh no, Mot thought, perhaps I should have done what Angelica and Asha told me. However, it's too late now; she's seen me with her own eyes talking and walking. I can't pretend to be a stuffed toy ever again.

Mot began to feel frightened. He started to walk back to Angelica's bedroom hoping to hide and be safe again. But he smelt fresh air and noticed the bedroom window in Mum and Dad's room was wide open. Mot saw Mum put first one foot then another on the stairs. And with that Mot, without a second thought, spread his wings and flew straight into Mum's bedroom and out through the window.

Mum stopped in her tracks, her mouth wide open in utter amazement and shock.

Mot flew, and as he flew he felt himself growing larger and larger, just like he had before.

Mum slowly climbed the stairs and walked into her bedroom and looked out of the window. She could hardly believe her eyes as she watched the dragon flying. He was looking much bigger than he had been in the house. He was flying round and round the garden, up and down.

"Wait till I tell the others," Mum said. "This is more fun than being at the fair." Then an amazing thought struck her. I wonder if I could ride on the dragon?

Mot could see Mum standing at the bedroom window. He decided he would keep flying as long as he could. It was the safest thing he could do now.

Whoopee!

"Don't fly away and leave us!" Mum shouted out of the window. "This is Dragon Cottage and you're our dragon."

Mot, still flying, wondered if it really would be safe to stop flying.

"Please don't go!" Mum shouted.

Mot wanted to stay more than anything.

Huh. That's not what Angelica and Asha said. They've been hiding me so I could stay. I wish I'd done what they told me to do and stayed under the bed. I wish I was safely there, right now. Mot wondered how he could fly back through the window and hide under the bed. But now Mum had seen him there was no chance of that.

Mum continued to look out of the bedroom window and Mot continued to fly.

"I'd like to fly with you but I haven't got wings like you!" Mum shouted.

Mum wondered what it would be like to be a dragon. What it would be like to fly, to be free and have fun. If only I could fly with Mot, she wished. Then she realised how silly her thoughts were. She was a grown up; a mum and a wife. But the thought kept whirring round in her head. This tiny dragon who had sat in the kitchen, that she thought was a toy, was now flying round and getting bigger and bigger in front of her eyes. If he can do that, I can fly too, on his back. With that she shouted out of the window. "Please will you stay here. I want to ride on you and fly."

And it was only then that Mot remembered the dream he had had. Someone had been riding on his back but he never knew who it was. C… c… could it have been Mum? he thought. Perhaps we're going to have an adventure together.

Mot's skin tingled with excitement. If Mum was really saying the truth he could go on an adventure, flying with her. His excitement outweighed his fears and it was not many minutes before he had landed on the lawn.

Mot couldn't believe what he was doing. He felt bigger than he'd ever been in his life, and now he was not only able to fly, but fly with Mum.

Mum, seeing him, ran down the stairs as fast as her legs could carry her. She ran out into the garden and jumped on Mot's back. Before either of them could think about what was happening, or could happen, Mum threw her oven gloves around his neck like a scarf and they were off.

Mot couldn't believe what he was doing, he felt bigger than he'd ever been in his life. Now he was not only able to fly, but fly with Mum on his back. Whoopee! This was fun, the best fun ever. If only Asha and Angelica could see him now.

They flew higher and higher, round and round whirling above Dragon Cottage. Mum held on to Mot but didn't feel frightened at all. She knew the dragon from Dragon Cottage had at last appeared and was real: very real indeed. She shrieked with delight. The more she shrieked the more excited Mot felt. He didn't care that his skin was not green all over. He didn't worry about anything until he heard familiar voices from far below shouting his name.

Angelica, Asha and Dad were looking up in horror as they saw not only the dragon flying, but with Mum on his back. What was that strange thing flapping around his neck?

Whatever do you think you're doing?

Asha looked at Angelica and Angelica looked at Asha.

"How did that happen?" Angelica whispered. "Why didn't he just stay under the bed?"

Before Asha could reply, Dad shouted out, "Whatever do you think you're doing? Come down here immediately."

Mum either couldn't hear his words or chose to ignore them. Mot began to feel frightened. What if Dad said he couldn't stay at Dragon Cottage? What would Angelica and Asha say because he hadn't hidden under the bed?

Mum was smiling and shouted, "I'm having more fun than you had at the fair."

"Whatever's come over her," Dad muttered. "Just come down here!" he shouted.

But Mum and Mot continued to fly over Dragon Cottage, over the garden and over their heads.

"Mot's got a scarf on," Asha whispered.

"Mot, who's Mot?" Dad asked.

"He's the dragon."

"What's he doing here? We thought he was a toy."

"He's a real live dragon. The dragon of Dragon Cottage. We've been hiding him because we were frightened you wouldn't let him stay."

"But he's too big to hide; look at him."

"He can grow as well as get smaller. I didn't know he could grow that big. Big enough for Mum to ride on him," Angelica said.

"Well, it looks like he can and that's my wife up there. I want her back. She may never come down. She may fall off," he said in horror.

But Mum was smiling. "Weeee!" she shouted as she flew over their heads.

"Tell Mot to come down here right now," Dad said. "She's uncontrollable and won't listen."

Then Mot spoke. The only person who could hear him was Mum. "I think we should land on the lawn now."

"No, no, I'm having far too much fun. More fun than I've had in my whole life." She tugged at the oven gloves around his neck. "Keep flying."

But Mot began to feel worried, a little frightened of Dad and the children. If he made them angry they may make him leave Dragon Cottage. "No, we're going to land," he said firmly to Mum. And with that he swooped down and gracefully landed on the lawn.

Mum lost her balance as he landed, mostly because she was angry that Mot had stopped her fun, and Dad ran forward to rescue her.

"Whatever's going on round here? You're a changed woman. We only left you while we went to the fair and look what you've got up to."

"Yes, I've been up, up and away," she laughed. "You should try it yourself."

Dad looked at her sternly. "And you should grow up and be sensible. Anything could have happened to you."

Then Mot spoke and everyone was silent. "She was quite safe with me."

"What else does this dragon do?" Dad asked.

"Time will tell," Asha muttered. "If only we knew."

Angelica smiled. "But Mot must stay here now. He's the real dragon of Dragon Cottage."

Mum said, "Of course."

Dad was not so sure. Mum unwrapped the oven gloves from around Mot's neck and put them back over her shoulder. She walked back towards the kitchen and Dad looked at her in astonishment.

Upside down and inside out

Dad stood on the lawn with his mouth wide open. He'd only taken the children for a fun time to the fair. While he was away his whole world had turned upside down. Upside down and inside out.

Mot looked at him and started to tremble. He knew he should have done what Angelica and Asha had told him: stay hiding under the bed. But sometimes a dragon has to do what a dragon has to do and he had done it. That's for sure. But what was going to happen to him now?

Asha and Angelica stood looking at Dad and Mot.

"He's so big he's never going to fit under the bed again," Angelica whispered.

But Asha was too worried what Dad was going to do now. "Thanks for taking us to the fair," he stuttered, trying to distract Dad's attention.

"If only we had stayed at home none of this would have happened," Dad said.

Mot felt sad. Then he felt himself getting smaller and smaller.

"Whatever's happening now?" Dad said, taking his glasses off and rubbing his eyes. "Is it my eyes?"

When Mot was much, much smaller he quickly ran towards Dragon Cottage and walked through the open doorway into the kitchen. Mum didn't even notice him.

Asha ran into the kitchen, scooped Mot up in his hands then ran helter-skelter up the stairs and put him under Angelica's bed. "Now stay there and don't move ever again."

Don't worry I won't, Mot thought, relieved to be back.

Angelica stood on the lawn with Dad. She looked up at his face wondering what was going to happen now.

"Am I seeing things? Am I imagining Mum was riding on that dragon? Tell me none of it is true," Dad pleaded.

"We do live in Dragon Cottage, so what did you expect? Thanks for taking us to the fair," Angelica said. Then she ran indoors to find Asha and Mot.

"Phew that was a close thing," Asha said when Angelica walked into her bedroom.

"Where is he?"

"Safely back under the bed."

"I can't believe Mum was riding on Mot."

"She looked so funny. I can't believe our Mum would ever do anything like that."

They began to giggle.

"It's our turn next," Angelica said.

Mot poked his head out from under the bed, grinning from ear to ear.

"Not now," Asha said. "You've caused enough trouble already. It's Dad I'm worried about. What's he going to do now?"

Mot slunk back under the bed. "I hope he'll let me stay here forever and ever."

"Just stay under the bed and don't move," Asha said seriously.

What if?

In the darkness and quietness of the night Mot, from his place back under the bed, began to feel restless. What if Dad says I can't stay now? What if... what if... what if I have another adventure.

Excitement overtook Mot's fear. He left his place under the bed and peered up at Angelica's window. It was tightly shut. He walked as quietly as he could to Asha's bedroom. This window was tightly shut too. He didn't know whether he dare walk into Mum and Dad's room. He peered through the doorway; it was very dark, but he could see the stars shining through the window. The open window. He felt a tingle of excitement. The same excitement he had felt when Mum was on his back shouting, 'Weeee! Keep on flying.'

I wonder if Mum wants to come for another adventure? But just at that moment, a very loud snore and snort jolted him back to reality. He rushed back into Angelica's bedroom. He knew the snore had come from Dad and he wasn't going to upset him any more.

Angelica heard the scuffling noise of Mot as he rushed back into her room. She rubbed her eyes again and jumped out of bed. "Oh no, what's he doing now?" she muttered.

And it was just at that moment Mot had, what he thought, was his best idea ever. If Mum can't come on another adventure I'll go with Angelica and Asha too if he wants. Then the strangest thing happened. Who should walk into the bedroom but Asha.

"What's going on, is something wrong?"

"Nothing's wrong, in fact everything is just right. I'm going on another adventure, want to come?"

"Oh no, can't you go back under the bed and just stay there. You've caused enough trouble as it is," Asha said firmly.

Angelica was intrigued. "What adventure?"

"How about coming for a ride? I did it with Mum; it was great fun."

Asha walked over to the curtains and peered out. "But it's dark."

"I know, but the stars are twinkling in the sky and look, the moon is shining very brightly."

Angelica started to feel excited but Asha felt worried.

"If Dad knows we've all gone he'll never let Mot live here. Never, ever."

"Of course he will, because we'll be back before it gets light. He'll never know."

Asha began to feel excited. "Are you sure we can do it? You're so small you'll have to grow."

"Just carry me downstairs and when we go outside I'll go for a quick fly round. When I'm flying I start to grow. I don't know how it happens, it just does. Then when I'm bigger I'll land on the lawn, you climb on board and we'll be off." Mot grinned.

"Promise we'll be back before breakfast."

"Yes, you'll be safely tucked up in bed and I'll be back under the bed. Mum and Dad won't be any the wiser. But I may be," he said wistfully.

Off on an adventure

Asha and Angelica stood on the lawn in their pyjamas, dressing gowns and slippers looking up at Mot flying above their heads.

"Do you think this is a good idea?" Asha asked.

Angelica giggled. "If Mum can do it, I'm sure we can."

"Suppose so," Asha murmured. "I'm just worried if Dad finds out he'll send Mot away."

As Mot flew he started to grow.

"How does he do that?" Angelica asked.

"I don't think anyone knows including himself. I wonder how big he can get? I wonder if he'll ever lose the rest of his flowery skin and be an all green dragon?"

The questions remained unanswered and Mot landed on the lawn in front of them.

"Jump on like Mum did."

Mot was just the right size for the children and they clambered on to his back.
"Hold on."

Angelica sat at the front and held on to Mot and Asha hung onto Angelica.

Mot took off, but as he did so he saw one of the upstairs curtains was pulled slightly back and a face pushed up against the window. He couldn't see if it was Mum or Dad, but he was too excited to worry. He was off, off on an adventure and taking Asha and Angelica with him. Mot flew and flew, round the garden, round Dragon Cottage and all was well until he was flying past the upstairs window. The upstairs window with Dad staring out at him.

Mot began to shake, shake and shake. Angelica and Asha felt frightened and held on very tightly.

"I knew we shouldn't have come," Asha shouted.

Mot was too worried about Dad and what Dad might do to him if he landed and tried to go back inside Dragon Cottage.

Somehow, the fairies in the tree house sensed a problem. Not knowing what it was one or two flew outside to investigate.

"Mot is flying, he's very big and the two children are riding on his back, but I think there's something wrong. Come on," one fairy said.

All the fairies gathered together and flew in Mot's direction.

Hang on tight!

Mot zoomed erratically up and down in the air, shaking with fear.

"Hang on tight!" Angelica shouted.

"Don't worry I am!" Asha shouted back, tightening his arms around her waist. "What's happening?"

"I wish I knew."

I should have stayed under Angelica's bed, Mot thought. But I don't think Dad will allow me back, now I've gone on another adventure and taking Angelica and Asha with me. Mot felt very, very frightened. The more frightened he felt the more he dropped downwards.

"We're going to crash, hold on!" Asha shouted.

"I'd rather jump off now!" Angelica shouted back.

"Don't be silly we're too high, just hang on tight."

Then Angelica saw some twinkling lights flying towards them. "Look, the fairies are coming."

"Where?"

"Over there."

"Are you sure?" Mot asked breathlessly.

"Yes, really, really sure."

Mot took a deep breath and he began to feel less frightened. His friends had come to rescue him.

"Hurry up," Angelica called hoping the fairies could hear her and fly even faster. "We need help."

Mot saw the twinkling light of a fairy out of the corner of his eye.

"Just keep flying like we taught you," she called.

Mot, hearing her tiny voice, began to shake with excitement.

"Oh no!" Asha shouted.

It was not many minutes before he was surrounded by more and more of his fairy friends.

"And where do you think you're going?" one of them called.

"I don't know, I just wanted another adventure and I wanted to take Asha and Angelica with me."

"So what went wrong?"

"I saw Dad's face at the window glaring at me and I'm sure he won't let me back in Dragon Cottage."

"Oh dear, oh dear, that is a big problem."

But however frightened Mot felt this time he didn't plunge up and down, or start to drop, much to Asha and Angelica's relief.

Faster, faster

"A problem shared is a problem halved," one of the fairies called to Mot. "We're going to stay with you now."

"That's good," Angelica called. "We thought we were going to crash."

The fairies whispered amongst themselves.

"We've decided a few of us will fly back to Dragon Cottage to see how Dad is and the rest of us will stay with you."

"Does that mean you're coming on an adventure with us?"

"Yes."

Mot flew faster and straighter than he'd ever flown. He felt happier than he'd ever felt. He was with all his friends now and hopefully the fairies who were flying back to Dragon Cottage could do something.

"Where are you going?" one of the fairies asked.

"I don't know, but it's going to be the best adventure of all adventures ever."

"Whoopee!" Asha called. "Faster, faster Mot, come on, you can do it."

Mot didn't need much encouragement, and with a sudden spurt of power he was off.

"Hold on tight," Angelica called to Asha. "We don't want you falling off."

"No, we certainly don't," one of the fairies said sternly. "Calm down, Mot. Don't forget you have two passengers on your back."

Mot flashed his teeth and smiled. "They've looked after me and I will look after them, don't worry."

"Where can we go?" Asha shouted with excitement.

"Dragonland," Mot replied suddenly. "I don't know where it is, but we're going to find it."

"Oh no," Angelica sighed. "We'll get lost."

"What happens in Dragonland?" Asha shouted.

"Hopefully, I'll be able to find out how I can be a proper green dragon."

"There must be an easier way," Angelica whispered to one of the fairies by her side.

"Don't worry, we're here with you all the way."

"Do you know where Dragonland is?" Angelica asked hopefully.

"No."

"So, no one knows, including Mot. I wish I was tucked up in my bed at home."

The fairy looked up at the stars twinkling high above them. "I'm sure everything will be all right."

"Hold on tight," Mot said, and then powered up.

"Hey, wait for us, we can't go that fast," the fairies called.

"I haven't any time to waste," Mot called.

"Oh no," Angelica whimpered. "This doesn't feel much like an exciting adventure to me."

Bubbling mud

A fairy kept repeating over and over again, "We're going to Dragonland. We don't know where it is, or what happens there, but we're all going."

Some of the other fairies heard her and joined in.

Angelica began to feel happier and joined in too. "We're going to Dragonland. We don't know where it is or what happens there but we're all going."

Mot was pleased that some of the fairies had flown back to Dragon Cottage. So when he returned from Dragonland he would be safe to fly back to Dragon Cottage and stay there… then a little thought sprung into his mind. Or perhaps we'll stay in Dragonland.

Mot flew with the children on his back and the fairies by his side. He was on the biggest adventure of his life.

The time and miles moved on and Mot somehow just felt deep, deep inside that he was near Dragonland. He didn't know how, but he just did. "I think we're nearly there."

"Oh good," the fairies called. "We're getting tired."

"Oh goodie!" Angelica shouted.

"So, you do know where Dragonland is," Asha called.

"Yes, I think I do. I don't know how, but I do. Hold on tight we're going to land soon."

Asha held on to Angelica and Angelica held on tightly to Mot. He circled round, slowly coming down nearer to landing as he did so.

The fairies kept very close to Mot, not knowing what was going to happen next, but somehow trusting him.

Asha and Angelica's noses began to twitch. They were flying towards a rather nasty smell. The smell of bad eggs, then they saw bubbling mud not solid earth beneath them.

"Oh no, what's Mot doing. He can't land here," one of the fairies shouted. "Our feet will get stuck and oh, that smell. Pheweee! Hold your noses and your toesies!"

Keep calm, you can do it

A large, green dragon looked up, hardly believing his eyes. A flowery and green skinned dragon was flying above his head with two children sitting on his back. There were lots of fairy lights twinkling round.

"I've never seen such a thing in my whole entire life, whatever next?" he muttered.

Mot slowed down ready to land.

"Don't land on the bubbling mud; you'll get stuck."

"Thank goodness for that," a fairy called.

"Keep going, follow me." The large dragon ran to a flat piece of land among some bushes.

Mot looked down and circled round. "But I can't, I can't. I'll get stuck in the bushes."

"Hold on tight," Asha called.

"We'll help you!" one of the fairies shouted. "Quick, make a circle in the air round the bushes then Mot can land in the centre."

The fairies flew as fast as they could and Mot slowed down.

"Keep calm, you can do it," the large dragon called.

Mot took a deep breath. The children held on as tightly as they could and Mot juddered. Then slowed down, then stopped right in the middle of the fairy circle.

"Well done. Where have you come from?" the large dragon asked.

"Dragon Cottage."

"What's that?"

But Mot was too exhausted and relieved to have solid land under his feet to reply.

"Do you think we dare get off?" Angelica whispered. "Do you think we're safe here?"

Asha looked at the big dragon. "He looks all right to me. Just a larger version of Mot, but green all over," he grinned.

Dragonland

Asha climbed off Mot, but Angelica stayed firmly on his back.

"What's that smell?" Asha asked.

The large dragon replied, "This is dragon country you're in."

"Do dragons smell then? Mot doesn't."

The dragon opened his large mouth, showing very large teeth. Asha began to feel scared, but instead of a roar, a deep loud laugh bellowed out.

Angelica just watched. The fairies stayed very close to her, either flying round or perched on Mot's neck.

"No, dragons don't smell, but we live here and there are bubbling mud pools. We like it."

"Phewee! I'm not sure I do. Smells like bad eggs or…" Asha giggled.

"This is a powerful land. The bubbling mud reminds us that the earth is alive and powerful like us."

"Do you b... b... breathe fire?" Angelica stuttered.

"Yes, we can."

"Oh no," one of the fairies whispered. "I don't think I like it here. Can we go home?"

"Do you really breathe fire?" Asha asked excitedly. "Show me."

"We only do it if we really need to, or if we have to defend ourselves."

"Oh go on, show me."

"No, we use our power, our fire sensibly, not to show off."

Asha felt a little silly.

"Doesn't your dragon breathe fire?" asked the large dragon.

"No," Angelica replied.

"It would be nice if I could, it would be nice if I was green all over like you. By the way, my name is Mot and this is Angelica and Asha."

"I'm Alfredo."

"And we're the fairies. There's lots of us; we're Mot's friends. Some of us went back to Dragon Cottage as there was a problem there."

"Is that why you wish you could breathe fire?"

Mot thought for a while. "I never knew I could." Then his mind started whirring. "If I could breathe fire just think what I could do. If I felt scared I could…"

"We dragons only find our power and our fire when we are grown up enough to use it properly. Just think what damage young dragons could do if they were breathing fire all over the place."

Asha laughed. "Sounds like fun to me."

"Shh," Angelica said.

A loud shuddering noise came from the trees behind the bushes. It got louder and louder.

Asha ran back to Angelica and Mot. He was going to climb onto Mot; then if the worst came to the worst and Mot took off he wouldn't be left behind.

The pearl

"Who's there?" a loud voice boomed.

"We have some visitors," Alfredo replied.

"I thought I heard some strange voices, so I'm coming to investigate."

Asha and Angelica held on tight to each other on Mot's back. "Mot, can you just take off?"

"I... I... I hope so, I'm not sure."

"Don't worry, we will help him," the fairies reassured. "Let's just see who it is first."

The branches swayed and twigs crackled as the owner of the voice came closer. Then a large head appeared. Larger than Alfredo's.

"It's... it's another dragon," Asha whispered.

"Just imagine if he breathed fire," one of the fairies shuddered.

"I'd rather not."

"But Alfredo did say dragons only use their fire sensibly."

"I hope he's right."

The large dragon eyed Mot up and down. "He's not a fully grown up dragon, look he's still got some flowery skin, and he's a lot smaller than us."

"He may be small but he's brave: he flew all the way here on his own."

"No, we were with him," one of the fairies called.

"And how did those children get here?"

"He flew with them on his back."

The large dragon went very quiet, then said, "I wonder why he did that?"

"I wanted an adventure," Mot replied, grinning. "We've come all the way from Dragon Cottage. I'm very pleased to see some more dragons like me. But I want to know how I will become green all over like you. I want everyone to love me. I want to become the dragon of Dragon Cottage and stay there forever."

"What's this Dragon Cottage?"

"It's our house," Asha said.

"We live there with Mum and Dad."

"I wished we had a dragon living in Dragon Cottage, then Mot appeared down Asha's bed. Just like that. But we had to hide him because we were worried Mum and Dad would say he couldn't stay."

"That's when he met us," one of the fairies said.

"Then Mum found me. I took her for a ride on my back when no one was around. She loved it and I was quite surprised but Dad was not pleased at all. Then I told Asha and Angelica I would not have any more adventures. I would stay hidden under their beds. But I just couldn't. The smell of fresh air tempted me on another adventure. The biggest adventure of my life. And here I am."

"Well done," the large dragon said. "Well done, and you managed to fly all the way here and you didn't get lost. You must be a most important dragon to be able to do that."

Mot shook his head with pride. "Well I never: a most important dragon."

Angelica put her arms round his neck.

"If only I wasn't flowery. I want to be a proper dragon."

"You are a proper dragon, a very proper dragon, just young. When you get older you will go green and when you get very old you'll grow a beard like mine."

The big dragon held his chin up.

"There's something glistening in his beard," Asha said. "Look."

"You can see my pearl."

"I haven't got one yet," Alfredo said. "It's only when you get old and wise."

Mot and the children just stared.

"I'm even getting used to the smell of Dragonland," Asha said.

"I'm not so sure I am," one of the fairies whispered.

Angelica just stayed silent.

We're off

"I think we should take them to meet some of the other dragons that live here," the large dragon said. "Would you all like that?"

"I'm not too sure," Angelica whispered.

"Me neither," a fairy replied.

"Will there be any more dragons who look like me?" Mot asked.

"But of course."

"Then I would. Can we go now?"

"I'm staying on Mot," Angelica said.

"If he goes, I go."

"I don't know whether he can walk with us on his back through these bushes."

"Oh dear, I feel safer up here."

Mot's eyes lit up with excitement. "We're going on another adventure to find a dragon like me."

"Oh no," Angelica said. "Not another adventure."

"Hold on tight. We're off."

"Follow me," the large dragon said, "Because I'm bigger than you. If you follow right behind I'll clear the way for you."

"And I'll follow behind to make sure the children are safe," Alfredo said.

With that they were off. Some fairies hanging onto Mot's neck and some flying by his side.

"I hope we're not going to end up nearer to the bubbling mud. Pheweee!" Asha said.

"No, don't worry."

And beyond the bushes and trees was a clearing with a large lake.

"Do dragons swim?" Angelica asked.

"No." Alfredo laughed. "But these are hot springs. Can you see the mist hovering over the water?"

"It looks quite magical," Angelica said. "I wonder if there are any fairies here?"

"It is magical. The hot springs come from deep, deep inside the earth, reminding us of our own power. We feel very comfortable here."

"Look over there!" Mot shouted, seeing a flowery skinned dragon.

"Over there also. There's a dragon who looks just like you."

Mot felt the happiest he had ever felt. "You see, my adventures have brought me to the right place. I did know what I was doing, even though no one thought I did."

Angelica and Asha were speechless.

Wise words

Mot walked over to the flowery skinned dragons, with Asha and Angelica still sitting on his back and the fairies sitting on his neck or flying around him.

"Do you feel different from all the other dragons?"

"No," one replied. "There are lots of us younger dragons. You can't be so young because you're partly green and must be very strong to carry passengers."

"I flew from Dragon Cottage with them. I don't live in Dragonland, but I always felt I wanted to be green all over, then I would be a proper dragon."

"We're proper dragons, just young ones."

"I wish someone had told Mot that before, then he wouldn't have felt so sad," Asha said.

"But we may never have had such exciting adventures. We have had lots of fun since Mot arrived." Angelica said, remembering pushing Mot up the ladder to the tree house, then meeting the fairies, then seeing him sitting on the chimney of Dragon Cottage. "Life has certainly been different since Mot arrived. And now we're all in Dragonland."

"But what about Mum and Dad? Do you think they're worried about us?"

One of the oldest dragons with a very large, shiny pearl in his beard looked down at them. "Don't worry, dragon time is different from human time. When you go home, although you've been away a long time, it's only a few minutes in the human world."

"How does that happen?" Asha asked.

"I may be old and wise, but I don't have the answer to that question. I've never been out of Dragonland."

Mot felt very surprised. "But how did I get there?"

"Someone must have made a wish for a dragon."

Angelica said, "I did, I really did."

"And that's why Mot was sent."

"So you really, really are our special dragon. Can he stay with us forever?"

"If he wants, but he can come back here too whenever he wants."

The wise old dragon looked down tenderly at Mot. "I can see you love being in Dragon Cottage and I can see everyone loves you too."

"Everyone except Dad."

"I think he's scared."

"Scared. Why?"

"I don't know." The wise old dragon touched his beard and his pearl, and began to think. Everyone was very quiet just watching and waiting.

Angelica broke the silence by saying, "Mum isn't scared of Mot, she loves having him at the cottage. She even went for a ride on him, but when Dad saw her riding on the dragon in the air, he became angry and frightened. When she shouted, 'Whoopeee' as she flew over his head, he said she's uncontrollable and won't listen."

"What did you do then, Mot?"

"I began to feel worried and frightened that Dad would say he wouldn't want me in Dragon Cottage, so I landed."

"Good. All young dragons like to have fun, but you need to know when to be sensible."

"But if I'd been that sensible, I would still be hiding under the bed and I wouldn't ever have had any adventures. And I wouldn't be in Dragonland now."

"I understand," the wise old dragon said smiling.

"I can see you like having adventures and you are very clever, but you have to think about others too. You did when you landed on the lawn with Mum. But you must understand it was a big shock to Dad."

"Yes, Dad had thought Mot was just a toy dragon," Asha said.

"So did Mum until we went to the Fair with Dad."

Mot began to wish he had a beard and pearl to touch when he was thinking. "I'm beginning to understand," Mot said quietly.

"Good, you're beginning to learn. I've been learning all sorts of things since I was your age."

"Were you ever little and flowery like me?" Mot looked up at the wise old dragon.

"Yes. I met a wise old dragon with a beard and a pearl and I remember asking him the same question."

"And what did he say to you?"

"Exactly what I'm telling you."

"I can understand why Dad was so angry and shocked now. I was far too busy having fun to think about how others felt."

The wise old dragon looked down at Mot tenderly, with big soft eyes full of love. "We all like fun."

"Even when you're old and wise?"

"Yes."

"Can you breathe fire?"

"Yes."

"Now?" Asha asked eagerly.

"No. I had to learn to use it wisely and not to hurt others." Then he smiled. "I was rather naughty and rebellious when I was younger and I got into trouble. It took lots of older dragons to train me until I began to understand. Then this naughty, rebellious dragon started to grow up and think about others and did lots of good things and I learnt from my mistakes and now here I am, a big wise dragon. I can hardly believe it myself."

"I want to be like you one day, but I would like to live at Dragon Cottage."

"You can."

"I hope Dad will let me. It's such a long journey back and I'm very tired now."

"It's because you're only little. We could help. Alfredo and I could come with you. The children could fly on his back and you could ride on mine."

"And we could have a ride too," one of the fairies said.

"Whatever will Mum and Dad say if they see us all flying in the sky?"

"We won't know till we get there," Alfredo said. "I'm looking forward to seeing Dragon Cottage."

"Could we go soon?" Mot said. "I'm feeling rather homesick."

Dragon time is different from human time

"You're such a brave dragon to have flown all this way!" Alfredo shouted as he soared through the skies with Asha and Angelica on his back.

"And clever to know where Dragonland is," the wise, old dragon who had Mot as a passenger sitting on his back, called.

"And don't forget us. Our little fairy wings flew all that way. It's much better having a ride home."

"There's Dragon Cottage down there; I can see it!" Mot shouted.

"Yes, Mum and Dad are in there," Angelica called in excitement. "I can't wait to tell them where we've been."

"Do you think that's wise?" Mot replied.

"Don't forget some fairies are in Dragon Cottage. I wonder what's happened."

"And don't forget time is different in Dragonland. They may not have missed you," the wise dragon said.

"I think if you can land near the woodland a little way away from the cottage that would be safest and then we can just walk back."

"Yes, if they see three dragons not just Mot, I can't imagine what they'll do," Asha laughed. "That may be the answer. Outnumbered by dragons."

"Don't forget I want to live here forever. We had better be cautious, very cautious."

"Yes, if you stay with the other dragons, Asha and I can walk in as if nothing has happened and we'll carry on as normal."

"We want to come," one of the fairies said. "To see what the others have been doing. And to tell them about our adventure."

"But Mum and Dad may see you."

"I don't think so. We're coming to make sure you're safe."

Angelica looked down at her pyjamas, dressing gown and slippers. "We could creep back into bed and Mum and Dad will never know."

"What about me?" Mot called. "I'm too big to get through the door now."

"You got smaller before, I'm sure you can do it again. Then we'll carry you up."

"But I don't want to be a small dragon again. I'm proud of myself. I've flown all the way to Dragonland and met other dragons now."

"You can choose," the old dragon said. "You can change size whenever you want, but you can't change your skin. It happens naturally as you get older."

"Then when I get very old and wise and have done lots of good things, I'll grow a beard and have a pearl just like you, won't I?"

"Yes."

"I don't want you to go yet," Mot said. "Will you stay for a while."

"Yes."

"You'll have to hide," Angelica said. "But you're too big to hide."

"Don't worry we're adult dragons: we can take care of ourselves."

Mot began to get smaller and smaller. "I'll go inside with Asha and Angelica and hide under the bed," Mot decided.

Mud on the floor

In the morning, Mum walked into Angelica's bedroom. She was fast asleep. Mum drew back the curtains.

"That's strange there's some mud on the floor near her slippers," she muttered. "I thought her dressing gown was hanging on the door last night not on the floor near her slippers. Oh well, strange things happen I suppose." Then she remembered riding round on the dragon. "Yes, they certainly do," she said, with a big grin on her face. "I wonder where he is now?" She looked round the room, but the dragon was nowhere to be seen.

Mum walked into Asha's room. He was fast asleep. She saw his slippers and dressing gown lying on the floor too. I wonder why both of their dressing gowns are not hanging up? she thought. She picked it up wondering whether the dragon was hiding underneath. No, he was not.

Mum pulled back the curtains. "Time to get up."

But there was no response. Mum walked down the stairs and into the kitchen.

"Have you calmed down after your ride on the dragon?" Dad enquired, hoping above all hope she was back to her old self.

"I wish I knew where Mot is."

Then Dad remembered looking out into the night sky and seeing a dragon flying. "I saw him flying last night."

"Where?"

"Up in the sky."

"Are you sure?"

"No, I thought I was, but when I went back to bed, I thought I saw little flashing lights flying round the bedroom. Then something like fairy dust sprinkled down all over the bed. Then I realised I must be feeling over-tired and seeing things that weren't there at all."

"Those children are tired this morning, not heard a peep. I pulled back the curtains, but still they didn't wake."

"There's no hurry is there, no school. Let's leave them alone and perhaps we can have a quiet breakfast together, just the two of us, and get back to normal."

Happy and content

Mot sat under the bed, thinking about his wonderful adventures. I promised them an adventure and I promised they would be back before breakfast. I don't know how I managed that, but I did. Then he remembered how his dragon friends had helped him and how happy and content he now felt. Flowery skinned or green, it didn't matter any more. If only he knew if Dad would let him stay in Dragon Cottage.

Asha rubbed his eyes, yawned and stretched. What a strange dream, he thought. It feels almost true. He walked into Angelica's bedroom; she was fast asleep.

"I've had the weirdest dream," Asha said.

"I'm tired, go away."

Then he decided to see if he could find Mot under the bed.

"Hello," Mot said. "Did you enjoy your trip to Dragonland last night?"

"I thought it was a dream."

"It most certainly was not."

Angelica heard Mot's voice and began to wake up.

'We've all been riding on Mot, except Dad," she said in a sleepy voice.

"He's the only one we're worried about," Asha replied.

"He's missed out on all the fun." Angelica smiled.

"You stay there, Mot, and we'll go downstairs and see Mum and Dad."

Angelica jumped out of bed and ran downstairs in her pyjamas.

Asha looked round the room: everything seemed quite normal, nothing to worry about at all and no fairies in sight.

Angelica studied Dad's face: he seemed calm and happy as if nothing had happened.

I hope Alfredo and the big, wise dragon haven't gone, Asha thought.

"There's nothing planned for today, is there?" he asked.

"No."

"Great," Asha replied, hoping they would soon go off to find Alfredo and the big, wise dragon.

No change

"I haven't seen any of the fairies," Mot said wistfully.

"No, neither have I," Asha replied.

"How did Dad look?"

"Dad looked like Dad, no change."

"Oh no," Mot said. "No change, so Dad won't want me living at Dragon Cottage now he's seen me taking Mum flying."

"No, I meant no change from before Mum's flight. Everything seems to have gone back to normal. It seems almost too good to be true," Asha said. "Perhaps he is just hoping everything will go back to how it was."

"I will go away, oh no…!" Mot began to look very sad.

"I think we need to find the fairies and talk to them. Perhaps they were able to do something while we were in Dragonland."

Mot's face brightened. "That's a very good idea. Now why didn't I think of that?"

"Let's get dressed quickly and look round the cottage to see if we can find the fairies."

"I'm coming with you," Mot said. "I'm small now, so Mum and Dad won't see me."

"No, no you stay here under the bed and we'll come back and tell you when we've found them."

"I want to see my dragon friends. They may fly back to Dragonland soon and I want to say goodbye."

"We'll be as quick as we can, just stay under the bed and don't move. Just don't."

Asha and Angelica were dressed in record time and then walked round Dragon Cottage, looking in every room.

"What are you two doing?" Dad called.

"Just wondering what to do today," Angelica replied.

"It's a nice sunny day, why don't you go and play outside?"

"Don't get into any mischief," Dad said, gazing at his wife hoping above all hope that she wouldn't either.

But Mum was cleaning the breakfast table as usual. "I think I'm going to spend some time weeding in the garden today."

"And I'll mow the lawn. Why don't you play in the tree house?" Dad suggested.

Why didn't we think of that? Asha thought. That's where the fairies will be. It was not many minutes before they were sitting in the tree house… alone.

"Where have they gone?" Angelica whispered. "They must be together somewhere because we haven't seen even one."

"You don't think they've all flown off to see the dragons?"

"Oh no, not to Dragonland."

"No, to the woods where Alfredo and the big, wise dragon are."

"Of course, why didn't we think of that before? Come on, let's go before Mum and Dad come in the garden and start asking questions about where we're going."

Asha and Angelica were down the ladder as quick as a flash and running out of the garden as quick as quick could be, completely forgetting about Mot under the bed.

Where can they be?

Asha and Angelica stood in the woods where Mot had landed… alone. No dragons and no fairies.

"Where can they be? I hope they've not all gone," Asha said.

Just then there was a loud shuddering noise from the trees behind the bushes. The branches swayed and the twigs crackled.

"That's them," Asha called excitedly.

First, the large dragon appeared, then Alfredo with all the fairies flying around them.

"So that's where you were," Angelica called.

"Where's Mot?" Alfredo asked.

"Oh no, he's under my bed."

"We want to say goodbye to him. We will be flying back to Dragonland soon. I don't think it would be wise if we went to Dragon Cottage to see him, so can he come to see us?"

Angelica sat cross-legged on the ground thinking.

"What shall we do?" Asha asked.

"Can we help?" one of the fairies asked.

"I don't know. I wish you could."

"Perhaps Mot could fly here?"

"Mum and Dad would see him; they're in the garden."

The cottage was quiet. Very,very quiet, and Mot felt restless. Asha and Angelica had been gone a long time and he wanted to see his new friends again before they returned to Dragonland. He crept out from under the bed and looked towards the window. It was tightly shut. But the smell of fresh air filled his nostrils. He slowly walked into Mum and Dad's room, but the window was shut. He wondered if he dared to stand on the landing looking down the stairs. The last time he had done that Mum had seen him. But he couldn't resist. He stood looking down and no one looked up. Most importantly the back door was wide open. Then he heard voices. The voices of Mum and Dad and ran as quickly as he could back to his safe place under the bed. I wish Asha and Angelica would come back soon to help me, Mot wished. I'm stuck here.

A little fairy flew into Angelica's bedroom. "I'm glad you're still here, I was worried you may have gone on another adventure," she teased.

"Of course not," Mot replied with a grin.

"The dragons will be flying back to Dragonland soon and want to say goodbye to you, but we don't know how to get you to them."

"All the windows are shut, but the back door is open. However, Mum and Dad are in the garden."

"Oh, so you have been trying to go on another adventure."

Mot suddenly realised what he had said. He chuckled. "They had been gone a very long time and what was I supposed to do?"

The fairy was speechless.

"Perhaps you could distract Mum and Dad in the garden to give me time to fly out of the back door and be gone."

"You won't know the way to the other dragons."

"I didn't know the way to Dragonland, but I found it. How will I know when it's safe to go?" Mot asked.

"I'll let you know, somehow."

It was not the right time

Mot sat at the top of the stairs looking down, waiting for some kind of sign that the fairy had distracted Mum and Dad. He listened carefully and after a while he couldn't hear Mum and Dad's voices any more. That must be it, he thought. Now's the time. I'm off. He flew down the stairs and out through the back door. He daren't stop and look around; he just flew.

But it was not the right time. Mum and Dad were standing talking at the end of the lawn… and saw Mot flying.

"There's that dragon again," Dad announced. "It's only small but I'm sure I saw it flying that way. Quick I'm going to follow it."

"Oh no!" Mum said.

"Oh yes!" said Dad running.

The fairy hearing and seeing Dad flew as fast as she could. This was an emergency. She didn't know what to do, but knew she had to do something, and quickly.

Mot circled over the trees hoping to see Alfredo.

"There he is, look." Angelica pointed. "How did Mot manage that?"

"I expect he'll tell us when he lands," Alfredo said. "He's much smaller than before."

"It's because he's been hiding under Angelica's bed. He's a lot bigger than he was earlier this morning."

Then they heard some twigs crackling and branches swaying and there stood Dad. He was rather out of breath. A few moments later Mum appeared with a very red face, puffing.

Dad stood back when he saw Alfredo and the big, wise dragon, not knowing what they might do to him.

Mot looked down horrified. Dad must have followed him and he had led them here.

Then he saw the little fairy flying near him. "I didn't give the 'all clear' sign," she gasped.

"I couldn't hear voices so I thought it was safe. What shall I do now?"

Dragon Cottage will be no more

"Could I go for a ride on you now?" Mum asked Alfredo. "I've had a wonderful time with Mot."

Dad put his head in his hands. Just as he thought things were going back to normal he saw not one but two dragons. These were much larger than Mot. He began to feel very frightened and outnumbered. He looked up in the air and saw Mot flying overhead. Asha and Angelica and worst of all, his wife, didn't look frightened of the dragons.

"I'm going back to the cottage," Dad said firmly. "Dragon Cottage." Then he realised what he had said. "A… a… rgh. Is there no escape from dragons? We'll have to move house so we can all have a normal life."

"Oh no!" Asha said. "We love Dragon Cottage and we love our dragons. We've been to Dragonland."

Angelica put her hand over his mouth. "Shhh."

"Oh, have you? I'd like to go too," Mum said. "Which one of you dragons will take me?"

"Oh no you're not; you're going absolutely nowhere," said Dad.

Mot didn't know what to do, but decided he was safer flying in the air. He may not be out of sight but he was out of reach. Dad's reach.

The big, wise dragon remembered that Mot had told him about Dad. He began to feel rather sad for him. I wonder what I can do? It seems the fairies who went back to Dragon Cottage weren't very successful. The big, wise dragon looked down at Dad.

It was too much for Dad and he was off. Back to the cottage as quickly as he could and hopefully, safety. If the others wanted to stay, they could. If the others wanted to ride on dragons AGAIN, including his wife, they would just have to. He didn't want any part of it.

Nothing is working with Dad, the big, wise dragon thought.

Dad was relieved to be back, even if the others hadn't come with him, but as he opened the door, he saw the name 'Dragon Cottage' and he shuddered. I know what I'll do, I'll take that down. Dragon Cottage will be no more. Hoping above all hope that the dragons would be no more.

Dragons are not welcome here

Mot flew up into the air.

"Oh no, what's he doing now?" Asha said.

The fairies flew around him.

"We can't fly," Mum said sadly. "So, we'll have to walk back to Dragon Cottage. Come on, you two."

Asha and Angelica followed Mum.

The Dragon Cottage sign lay on the ground by the door. Mum stepped over it. "And what do you think you're doing?"

"This is not Dragon Cottage any more, can't you see? Dragons are not welcome here. We're going back to normal. There's going to be no more flying round here... ever."

Mum remembered the big, wise dragon's words and said nothing. She knew this was Mot's home and nothing Dad said would change that.

Dad was rather surprised by Mum's silence.

"And where are those dragons now?"

"Oh, they've flown back to Dragonland."

"That's the best thing I've heard for a very long time."

Mum didn't say that Mot hadn't gone with them.

Asha and Angelica sat in the garden, looking at Mot and the fairies flying above them. "I hope Dad doesn't come outside and see Mot."

"He could live in the tree house for a while," Angelica said.

"That's brilliant," Asha replied.

Somehow the fairies and Mot must have thought the same thing at exactly the same time.

Mot and the fairies all flew into the tree house.

"Do you remember when we had to push Mot up the ladder?" Angelica said.

"Yes, that seems like a long time ago and now he flies there himself."

"And we've been to Dragonland."

They ran over to the tree house and up the ladder. Mot was curled up and closing his eyes.

"He's going to have a sleep now," one of the fairies called.

"Us too," one yawned.

"Just stay here," Angelica said.

But they both knew Mot would do whatever he wanted, whatever they said.

"Let's go into the cottage and see what's happening."

"Yes, Mot seems settled."

He opened an eye as they left then fell into a deep sleep.

I never want to see another dragon

Asha and Angelica stepped over the Dragon Cottage sign and walked into the kitchen. Mum was sitting at the kitchen table having a cup of tea, while Dad was pacing up and down looking very angry. He didn't even notice them walking into the kitchen.

"I never want to see another dragon as long as I live. I've seen quite enough of dragons and seeing you riding on a dragon was the silliest thing ever."

Mum kept quiet. Asha and Angelica felt sad. They wanted Mot to stay in Dragon Cottage forever. They walked out of the kitchen completely unnoticed by Dad. They slowly climbed the ladder into the tree house. It was very quiet; all the fairies and Mot were fast asleep.

But one fairy was not asleep and saw their sad faces. She flew very close, but they still didn't notice her. She flew even closer to Angelica's face, who still did not see her. So she landed on her nose.

Asha started to giggle.

"What are you laughing at?" Angelica said.

"You look so funny with a fairy perched on the end of your nose."

"I haven't."

"Yes, you have."

The fairy fluttered her wings. "I'm here. You must be very tired. I couldn't get your attention whatever I did."

"I'm worried about Dad," Angelica replied. "He doesn't ever want to see another dragon."

"Don't worry I'll help you. I'll fly over to the cottage and check what's happening. They won't see me."

"Don't land on Dad's nose." Asha laughed, feeling relieved that the fairy may be able to help them.

"I'm glad Mot is sleeping. We don't want him to feel unwanted and fly back to Dragonland."

It's a bit late now

The fairy flew in through the back door, as Mum walked out of it.

Ah that's good, the fairy thought. I'll be alone with Dad and can see what's really happening. But Dad walked out of the back door too and picked up the sign saying Dragon Cottage. "That's the end of that," he muttered and threw it next to the dustbin. Then he walked back into the kitchen very quickly with the fairy just behind him. He sat down at the kitchen table and put his head in his hands. His face was covered and the fairy wished she could see what was happening. She stayed very close to him.

"Those dragons have changed my life forever. I just want it to go back to how it was," he muttered, and as he took his hands away from his face the little fairy saw some tears rolling down his face and go plop onto the table.

"Oh dear, oh dear, I need to help him." She flew back to the tree house to report to Asha and Angelica what was happening. Mot was still asleep when the fairy talked to the children.

"I've never, ever seen Dad cry before," Asha said.

"Perhaps everything was better before Mot arrived. Perhaps I should never have wished for a dragon to come to live in Dragon Cottage with us."

"It's a bit late now. And we have been to Dragonland and Mum has been for a ride on Mot. None of that would have happened."

"If Dad went for a ride on Mot, he may change his mind."

"He'll never do that. Dad never wants to see a dragon again."

Mot opened an eye. "What was that I heard?"

"Oh nothing," Angelica said quickly.

This isn't Dragon Cottage any more

Mum walked into the kitchen to see Dad sitting at the table looking very sad, not angry, but sad. Then Mum noticed a tear in his eye. "Have you got a cold, dear?" she asked.

Dad wiped the tear away quickly. "What made you think that?"

"Your eyes look like they are running."

But before Dad could reply another tear welled up and ran down his cheek, then another and another.

Mum had never, ever seen Dad like this before in all the years they had been married. "Are you sickening for something?" she asked putting her arm round his shoulder.

"I feel like my whole life has changed and… and… it's all because of those dragons. This isn't

Dragon Cottage any more, I've taken the sign down. It's a silly name anyway."

Mum went very, very quiet. "I rather like it."

"You like dragons and I don't. I just can't believe my eyes any more. First a toy dragon arrives. Then, while I'm out with the children at the fair, this toy becomes a real dragon, getting larger by the minute. Then, I come home and see you flying in the air on a real dragon and you're having the time of your life. Then, I hear my children telling me they've been on the dragon to Dragonland. And then horror of horrors, two more dragons appear, bigger than ever. I can't cope any more. All my family seem to think this is normal, including you. Am I going mad?"

Mum put her arm round him. "I suppose it does look very strange. I never thought about it like that. I was too excited."

There was a loud knock at the front door.

"I'll answer it," Mum said. "You stay there and drink your tea."

As Mum opened the door, she saw a man and a woman standing there. "Who are you?" she asked.

"This is er… er… Dragon Cottage isn't it? I can't see the sign," the man said.

"Yes."

"I knew it, I knew it. This must be where those dragons are coming from."

"What dragons?" Mum asked going red in the face.

"We saw two dragons flying in the sky above our house. We couldn't believe our eyes. Where were they coming from? Where were they going? We thought we were imagining it. Then we remembered Dragon Cottage and thought you must know. No one else would, except you."

Mum's face went even redder. "This isn't called Dragon Cottage any more. It's just called the Cottage in the Woods."

"When did that happen? It was always named Dragon Cottage," the woman said.

"You need to ask my husband."

"Can we speak to him?"

"No, he's not very well at the moment."

"It would be wonderful if there really were dragons here. And it was named Dragon Cottage," the woman said.

When Dad heard voices saying, 'it would be wonderful if there really were dragons here', he stood up and walked towards the door.

"I'm glad you think it would be wonderful because I certainly don't. I thought one was bad enough but three is too much for anyone."

"So, there are dragons here. We knew it. Where are they now?" the man exclaimed.

"They've gone back to Dragonland, wherever and whatever that is."

"D… D… Dragonland?"

"Yes, that's what I said."

"This was always called Dragon Cottage, not the Cottage in the Woods, when did that happen?" the woman protested.

"When I saw three dragons, I tore it down and threw it by the bin. No more dragons here, I never want to see another dragon," Dad said.

"We do," they chorused.

"You sound like my wife and children. I don't, can't you hear me?" Dad was just about to slam the door shut. "I've been outnumbered by dragons. Everyone seems to like them except me. Now go away and you can take that Dragon Cottage sign with you, if you like, then they may move into your house."

"No, you can't take the sign," Mum said, stamping her foot.

A tear rolled down Dad's face. He turned around so no one could see how upset he was. He walked back to the kitchen.

"We're very sorry."

"I need to be with my husband," Mum said and slowly shut the door.

What now?

Mum looked at the Dragon Cottage sign lying on the ground. She carried it into the kitchen. "No one is taking that anywhere. We are Dragon Cottage and that is what we will remain – forever."

Dad looked at Mum bringing it in. "If that's coming in, I'm going out." And with that, he walked into the garden. I know where I'll go to get some peace, in the children's tree house. No more dragons for me, he thought.

Asha heard Dad climbing the ladder.

"Oh no, quick hide, Mot."

"Hello, Dad. Have you come to see us?"

Dad thought for a moment. "I just wanted some peace to get away from dragons. Some people saw two dragons flying in the sky and believed they were coming from Dragon Cottage. I never want to see another dragon."

Mot slunk down further into his hiding place. Then he remembered the wise, old dragon's words: 'Dad is probably frightened as well as angry.' I'm frightened and so is Dad, Mot thought. What now?

The fairies were flying round the tree house listening. Asha and Angelica could see them. One flew very near to Dad, wafting her wings over his head. Asha smiled. Perhaps the fairies could come to the rescue. A little fairy winked at Asha, then waved her wand sprinkling fairy dust over Dad.

"That's strange I remember looking out of the bedroom window and seeing a dragon flying, or thought I did. Then I saw twinkling lights flying round the bedroom sprinkling something like fairy dust over the bed. I thought I must be over-tired and seeing things. But I'm seeing twinkling lights again in here. Perhaps it's all been too much."

Asha took a very deep breath, then taking a big risk said, "There are fairies in the tree house; this is where they live."

Angelica was horrified to hear his words.

"I can see twinkling lights, but I can't see any fairies," Dad said.

"The twinkling lights are fairies."

"They're better than dragons," Dad said. "Dragons frighten me, particularly when one took

Mum for a ride. Then there were three; that was just too much. I like the toy dragon we had, but I don't like real dragons."

Mot decided in that moment if Dad found him, he had to keep so still he would just think he was a toy.

"Would you like to go for a ride on a dragon?" Asha asked.

"Certainly not."

The fairies were flying all around Dad, sprinkling more and more fairy dust.

I wished for a dragon

Mum stood in the garden, wondering where Dad had gone. Then she heard voices coming from the tree house. Surely he's not up there, she thought. But the nearer she went she was sure she heard Dad's voice talking to the children.

She climbed the ladder carefully. "So, there you are." She noticed twinkling lights round Dad. "What's going on?"

"They tell me fairies live in here."

"Fairies," Mum repeated.

"Yes, I prefer them to dragons," Dad said seriously.

Mum just stood staring, not knowing what to think any more.

"You can't ride on fairies: they're too small," Dad said firmly.

Then Mum started to laugh. "Strange things have been happening here in Dragon Cottage lately, so you can never be too sure."

"I can," Dad said. "Fairies are real and they don't change size like that dragon did."

"Did you say real?" Mum asked. "Am I hearing things? I didn't know you believed in fairies."

"I didn't. They don't frighten me, but when I saw you flying round over my head on that dragon, that I had thought was a toy, well…" his voice trailed off.

"That was the most fun I've had for years. You should try it."

"Certainly not."

Mot was listening to the conversation carefully from his hiding place. Asha looked over to see he was safely hidden.

"I wished for a dragon to live in Dragon Cottage," Angelica said slowly. "You told me to be careful what I wished for. But I wanted a dragon, a real dragon to live here, and my wish came true."

"Oh, so that's how it happened," Mum said. "I couldn't understand where he'd come from."

"But we don't want any more dragons. One is not too bad, but three, two of them even larger, is too much for anyone."

"Two of them have flown back to Dragonland."

"I thought they had all flown back," Dad said. "Do you mean to say one is still here?"

There was complete silence.

Mot began to shake and shiver. Oh no, what's going to happen now?

Please don't make him go

"Where is the dragon?" Dad asked. "The one you were riding on."

"I don't know," Mum replied.

Dad looked at Asha and Angelica. "So, where is he?"

There was a long silence.

"Do you know?"

There was an even longer silence.

"No one is telling me anything?"

"We're not telling you until we know Mot will be safe and he can stay here. I wished for a dragon to live in Dragon Cottage and you just can't send him away now."

Dad looked sad. "I don't know what to say any more."

"Will you promise me you will never ride on that dragon again?" Dad asked Mum.

There was a very long silence.

Mot was trembling and waiting to hear what was going to happen next.

"I don't think I can say I will never ride on him again. That is, when we find him. Why don't you have a ride? You will understand how exciting it is then."

Asha and Angelica looked at Dad wondering what would happen next.

The fairies sprinkled some more fairy dust and waited.

"Shall we go back into the cottage?" Mum asked.

"I like it here," Dad replied. "I never realised this tree house was so nice before."

"You made it for us," Angelica said.

"We love it."

"Mot does too," Asha said. The words tumbled out of his mouth before he could stop them.

"Don't tell me Mot is here, in this tree house?"

Angelica went bright red and Asha looked down at the floor.

"Is he?" Mum asked.

"Come on, tell me," Dad said.

Mot had heard the conversation and didn't want Asha and Angelica to have to lie to protect him. There was a rustle from in the corner. Mot walked out from his hiding place. "Here I am."

"Have you been in here all the time I have? And I thought this place was free of dragons."

"Sorry," Mot said. "If you don't want me to stay in Dragon Cottage, I can go back to Dragonland. Alfredo and the big, wise dragon said I could. I'm sure I'll find my way back there." Then a large tear plopped onto the floor.

Dad's heart began to melt when he saw Mot was crying, just like he had done.

Angelica put her arms round Mot's neck and Asha walked nearer to Dad.

"Please don't make him go. He's the dragon of Dragon Cottage."

Can I stay here?

Dad said nothing for a very long time.

"Does this mean I've got to put the Dragon Cottage sign back up?"

Mum smiled.

"What do you mean, Dad? Can he stay?"

"I think I can just about cope with one dragon, our dragon, the dragon you wished for Angelica, but only one."

"The other two have really gone back to Dragonland," Angelica said.

Dad looked around the tree house. "Are you sure?"

"Yes. Those people who knocked on the door saw two dragons flying in the sky. They were on their way back to Dragonland."

"Oh yes," Dad said, remembering.

"In that case, Mot can stay, but I don't want to come home and find Mum riding in the air on our dragon."

"Our dragon?"

Dad smiled.

"I won't ride on Mot again, until after you have," Mum said, grinning.

"You may have to wait a very, long time then."

Mot looked up at Dad, another tear falling down his face and plopping onto the floor. This time tears of happiness. "Can I stay here all my life until I become a wise, old dragon and grow a beard and a pearl?"

"Yes," Dad replied. "Perhaps I'll grow a beard and have a pearl when I get old."

"Only dragons do, but you never can tell," Mot replied. "I only grow my pearl when I've grown older and done lots of good things and learnt from my mistakes."

"First, I need to put up the Dragon Cottage sign so everyone can see it, but I think I'll stay in this tree house a little longer. It's really rather nice."

The fairies twinkled as they flew above them.

"Perhaps the fairies would like to come into the cottage too. They might like it."

"They come all the time," Angelica laughed.

"Perhaps we should call it Dragon and Fairy Cottage. That would surprise any visitors who come. One day I think I may surprise everyone when they see me flying in the air on Mot, but I may surprise myself most of all."

Angelica and Asha laughed and happiness filled the tree house and Dragon Cottage. More happiness than anyone imagined possible.